STUCK IN

"You're in quite a rush, ain't you?" Longarm leaned forward a little, knowing that would probably force the tall, raw-boned man to move back. It did. He wondered if Emmaline was making a break for it. She might be, but he kept his eyes fastened on the man in front of him.

"Please," the man said, "I must get by." The man's temper was slipping away from him. He bulled forward, trying to shoulder past Longarm.

Longarm put a hand in the middle of the man's chest and shoved hard.

"You do not understand," the man said. He pointed a shaking finger past Longarm. "She is a thief! And she is getting away!"

Longarm finally glanced over his shoulder and saw that the man was right about one thing: Emmaline Colton was slipping through the door at the front of the car. She threw one frightened look back at the confrontation in the aisle, and then she was gone.

Longarm turned his head back toward the foreigner, just in time to see a knobby-knuckled fist coming right at his face . . .

**DON'T MISS THESE
ALL-ACTION WESTERN SERIES
FROM THE BERKLEY PUBLISHING GROUP**

THE GUNSMITH by J. R. Roberts
> Clint Adams was a legend among lawmen, outlaws, and ladies. They called him . . . the Gunsmith.

LONGARM by Tabor Evans
> The popular long-running series about U.S. Deputy Marshal Long—his life, his loves, his fight for justice.

SLOCUM by Jake Logan
> Today's longest-running action Western. John Slocum rides a deadly trail of hot blood and cold steel.

BUSHWHACKERS by B. J. Lanagan
> An action-packed series by the creators of Longarm! The rousing adventures of the most brutal gang of cutthroats ever assembled—Quantrill's Raiders.

TABOR EVANS

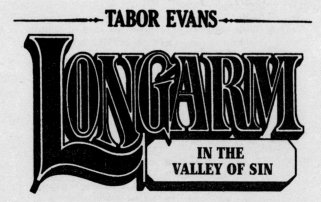

IN THE
VALLEY OF SIN

JOVE BOOKS, NEW YORK

This is a work of fiction. Names, characters, places, and incidents are either the product of the author's imagination or are used fictitiously, and any resemblance to actual persons, living or dead, business establishments, events or locales is entirely coincidental.

LONGARM IN THE VALLEY OF SIN

A Jove Book / published by arrangement with the author

PRINTING HISTORY
Jove edition / December 1999

The Penguin Putnam Inc. World Wide Web site address is http://www.penguinputnam.com

ISBN: 0-515-12707-8

A JOVE BOOK®
Jove Books are published by The Berkley Publishing Group, a division of Penguin Putnam Inc., 375 Hudson Street, New York, New York 10014.
JOVE and the "J" design are trademarks belonging to Penguin Putnam Inc.

PRINTED IN THE UNITED STATES OF AMERICA

10 9 8 7 6 5 4 3 2 1

Chapter 1

Lady Margaret Wingate lay facedown on the big, soft, four-poster bed and writhed her naked hips back and forth. "Punish me, Custis," she gasped into the pillow she was clutching frenziedly. "Now, my darling, hurry! And don't spare the lash!"

Longarm looked down at the short whip he was holding in his right hand. He was naked, just like Lady Margaret, and the sight of her unadorned blond loveliness wiggling around on the bed had a definite effect on him. His manhood was standing up at attention, a long, thick, heavy pole of flesh that was ready, willing, and able to plunge into the pink slit that winked invitingly at him from between her thighs. Warm yellow lamplight reflected off the dewy droplets of moisture that beaded the triangle of fine-spun blond hair adjacent to the cleft of her femininity.

Lady Margaret wasn't interested in the normal sort of romping, though. It took something else to get her all fired up.

"Please, Custis," she moaned. "Don't make me wait any longer!"

With a sigh, Longarm looked from her to the whip and

back again, then lifted it, poised to strike the first blow.

He wondered how the hell he managed to get himself into messes like this.

It was all Billy Vail's fault, of course.

"He's waiting for you," Henry had said with a smirk when Longarm entered the outer chamber of the chief marshal's office in the Federal Building on Denver's Colfax Avenue a few days earlier. "And he's not happy."

Henry was, though. The pasty-faced young man who played the typewriter for Marshal Vail had a long-standing feud with Longarm. Not that they were mortal enemies or anything like that, but Henry wasn't above enjoying the prospect of U.S. Deputy Marshal Custis Long getting a good ass-chewing from the boss.

Longarm didn't look particularly worried, though, and that reaction took some of the wind out of Henry's sails. The tall, rangy deputy stopped just inside the door and fished a cheroot out of his vest pocket. He wore a brown tweed suit, a white shirt, a string tie, and black boots. A Colt .44 with walnut grips rode in the holster that was canted slightly forward on his left hip for a cross-draw. Longarm's flat-crowned, snuff-brown Stetson was cocked at a rakish angle on his thatch of brown hair, and the tips of his sweeping longhorn mustache were freshly waxed. He was aware that he looked sort of like a dandy, but he didn't care. He'd just come from the barbershop, and the smell of bay rum clung to his cleanly shaven jaw.

Longarm felt good, damned good, and nothing Henry could say or do was going to ruin that for him.

Now, Billy Vail was another story, but Longarm had always been a firm believer in eating the apple one bite at a time. He'd get around to talking to Billy soon enough.

He hung his Stetson on the hat tree, then snapped a lucifer to life on an iron-hard thumbnail and held the flame to the tip of the cheroot. When he had it going good, he shook out the sulfur match and dropped it on the floor, knowing that would add to Henry's irritation. "You don't say," he drawled finally.

"I do say," snapped Henry. "You'd better get in thereo right now before things get any worse. If Marshal Vail hears your voice and comes out here to find you lollygagging, it'll go hard for you."

"Usually takes more than that to make it go hard," Longarm said with a grin, and was rewarded by the embarrassed flush that spread over the young clerk's face.

He had harangued Henry enough, Longarm decided. He took another puff on the cheroot and then ambled over to the door of the inner office. He knocked once, then opened the door and stepped inside.

Chief Marshal Vail glanced up from the welter of papers spread out on his desk. He was so plump and pink now that a casual observer would never guess he had once been a hard-riding lawman himself. His spectacles had slid down to the end of his nose. He pushed them back up and grunted.

" 'Bout time," he said. "We try to keep regular office hours around here, Custis. Reckon you ought to know that by now, since I've been telling you for years."

"I know, Billy," Longarm said as he lowered himself into the old red leather chair that sat in front of Vail's desk. He used the cheroot to point at the banjo clock on the wall of the office. "But it's only twenty minutes after nine, and I had to stop for a shave. Wouldn't want me coming in to work looking all grizzled and disrespectable, would you?"

Vail didn't answer that question. Instead, he picked up a piece of paper and slapped it down at the front edge of the desk, within easy reach of Longarm. "Read that."

Longarm picked up the paper and scanned it as he puffed on the cheroot. "Briarcliff Manor," he said. "Never heard of the place. Sounds like something out of one of Miss Austen's novels."

"Who?"

3

"Jane Austen—" Longarm stopped abruptly. It was bad enough for his reputation as a rough-and-tumble lawman that he liked to haunt the Denver Public Library—especially towards the end of the month when his funds were usually low and he couldn't afford the more expensive forms of entertainment—but he didn't want to go admitting that he'd ever read novels by genteel little English gals. When he went on, he said harshly, "And who the hell's this Brundage hombre?"

"Alfred Brundage. Sir Alfred, according to that report," said Vail. "Some sort of English doctor and scientist. I never heard of him either until today."

Longarm's eyes narrowed. He'd had a run-in with a British lord a few years back when the gent had come to Texas to hunt a so-called monster. That little dustup had come nigh to getting Longarm killed a few times, and he didn't have too many fond memories of Englishmen.

"What's he doing over here?" asked Longarm.

Vail pointed at the paper in Longarm's hand. "It's all right there, how he's built himself a damned castle down in the Sangre de Cristos."

"Briarcliff Manor," said Longarm.

"Yep."

"What's that got to do with us? How come Uncle Sam's interested in some Brit and his castle, even if it is in Colorado instead of over yonder in Sussex or Wessex or wherever the hell it is they're supposed to build castles?"

Silently, Vail picked up another piece of paper and extended it toward Longarm. The deputy marshal read it quickly, then looked up and said, "Aw, hell, Billy. Not another one of those nursemaiding jobs."

"What do you want me to do, ignore a direct request to the Justice Department from the Secretary of State? Brundage is having trouble, and he's asked the United States to look into it and help him out." Vail leaned back in his chair and pointed a finger at Longarm. "And in this case, Custis, *you* are the duly appointed representative of the United States of America."

"I don't get any choice in the matter?"

Vail shook his head. "Not a damned bit."

Longarm sighed. Much of his good mood had evaporated in the face of this new assignment he was being given. It was difficult for him to believe that he had been so jaunty just a few minutes earlier. Looked like ol' Henry was going to have the last laugh after all.

"All right, Billy," Longarm said. "I'll go down to the Sangre de Cristos and see what this Brundage fella's problems are." He scraped back the chair and started to stand up.

"Hold on," said Vail. "That's not all of it."

Longarm froze, halfway up out of the chair, then slowly lowered himself back into it. "What's the rest?" he asked grimly.

Vail picked up another piece of paper. "Seems like I'm asking you to do almost as much reading today as you'd find in one of those novels by Jane Austen," he said dryly.

Longarm grimaced and leaned forward to reach across the desk and snatch the paper from Vail's hand. His frown grew darker and darker as he read. When he finally looked up at the chief marshal again, he said, "A politician's son." The words sounded like they tasted bad in his mouth.

"That's right," Vail said with a nod. "Senator Hanley's boy, Mark. He's going to be one of Sir Alfred's guests too, and the senator would take it kindly if you'd keep an eye on him, sort of help him stay out of trouble."

"Trouble," said Longarm with a grunt. "You mean like what's written on this here piece of paper? Busting up saloons and paying off gals he slaps around and damned near beating a gent to death with a walking stick? That the kind of trouble you're talking about, Billy?"

Vail blew his breath out and laced his fingers together across his ample middle. "The lad's had a few brushes with the law," he admitted.

"A few brushes with the law!" Longarm waved the paper around. "Hell's fire, Billy, if his daddy wasn't an important man in Washington, Mark Hanley would've been in jail where he belongs a long time ago!"

Vail straightened in his chair and said, "You're right, he's a no-good bastard. You know it, I know it, and I reckon the senator probably knows it too. But Senator Hanley's still his father, and he doesn't want Mark getting into any more trouble. You're going to see to it that he doesn't."

"So this really *is* a nursemaiding job."

"Call it what you want," Vail said with a shrug. "Just go down there and take care of it." He started shuffling other papers around, indicating that the conversation was over. "Pick up your travel voucher and expense money from Henry."

Longarm's teeth clamped down on the nearly forgotten cheroot. That little weasel was going to get a real kick out of handing over Longarm's travel papers. He folded the documents Vail had given him and stuck them in an inner coat pocket to study some more later. As he stood up, he said, "I'll do my best, Billy."

"I know that, Custis. You didn't even have to say it." Longarm turned toward the door, and Vail cleared his throat, then went on. "There's just one more thing. . . ."

Longarm looked back over his shoulder, wary. "What's that?"

"You're not a deputy marshal anymore."

"A hardware salesman," Longarm muttered under his breath as he settled back in one of the seats about halfway along the aisle in this passenger car. "Couldn't Billy have come up with something better than that?"

For a minute, he thought about discarding the phony identity he had been told to use. After all, if he was pretending to be somebody else, why couldn't he be somebody dashing, like an explorer or some such? But no, Longarm realized, Sir Alfred Brundage had been told that the federal

6

lawman coming to investigate his troubles would be working in secret and posing as a hardware salesman named Custis Parker. So he was pretty much stuck with that identity.

Longarm wasn't sure why it was necessary for him to be working in secret on this job in the first place. It seemed pretty straightforward to him.

As the train lurched into motion and rolled out of the Denver & Rio Grande depot, headed south toward Trinidad and the Sangre de Cristo Mountains along the border between Colorado and New Mexico Territory, Longarm took out the papers Billy Vail had given him and began to read them over again.

According to these reports, Sir Alfred Brundage was not only a scientist, he was a medical doctor too, and he had come to the United States from England to take advantage of the high, dry, mountain air and test out some of his pet theories. Briarcliff Manor was what the Swiss called a spa, a place where sick folks could come to get well. Originally, it had been a ranch, but when Brundage had bought the place he'd had it rebuilt to look like an English manor. So it wasn't really a castle at all, Longarm supposed.

Brundage had been in business there for six months, and in that time, the place had gotten a reputation among high society and political circles. The rich, famous, and powerful came to Briarcliff Manor to get over whatever ailed them. Brundage claimed that his regimen of mineral baths, massage, and herbal potions and nostrums could cure anything from nervous conditions to stomach ailments to fainting spells. It sounded like quackery to Longarm, but evidently Brundage's methods had had enough success to attract patients from all over the country.

Mark Hanley, Senator Hanley's son, was one of them. He was due to arrive the day after Longarm, and one of Longarm's chores would be to see that the young rapscallion didn't get into any hot water—except for those mineral baths.

That was just a bonus, though. Longarm's real job was to find out who was trying to kill Sir Alfred.

That could be putting it a mite strongly, he told himself as he flipped through the reports. Brundage wasn't absolutely *sure* somebody was trying to murder him . . . but there had been several suspicious incidents of late that could have easily had fatal consequences. Not only that, but it seemed that some of the local citizens had a grudge of some sort against the scientist and the folks who came to Briarcliff Manor. There'd been some agitation among folks in the nearby town of Trinidad about how the place was a cesspool that ought to be cleaned out. Brundage attributed that to prejudice against him because he was a foreigner. He'd wired the British embassy in Washington asking for help, and the embassy had contacted the U.S. State Department, and so on down the line until responsibility for sorting out the whole mess had fallen on the shoulders of one Custis Long.

Or Custis Parker, rather, hardware salesman from Kansas City. The more Longarm thought about that, the more he was convinced that in his lack of imagination Billy Vail bad made a serious mistake. Any place as fancy and highfalutin as Briarcliff Manor seemed to be would charge fancy and highfalutin prices for its services. Prices a simple hardware salesman couldn't ever hope to afford. Longarm frowned and chewed on an unlit cheroot as he also chewed on this problem. Billy might not like it, but Longarm was convinced he was going to have to shoot from the hip on this one and change his story. As long as he got a chance to explain things to Sir Alfred early on, that ought not to cause too big a problem.

"Excuse me, do you mind if I sit down?"

The soft, musical, female voice yanked Longarm right out of his reverie. He turned his head, looked up, and saw a mighty attractive young woman standing there in the aisle, next to the empty seat beside him. She was about twenty-five, he judged, with curly auburn hair that fell around her shoulders. She wore a bottle-green traveling suit and a hat of the same shade with a small feather attached to it. Longarm came to his feet. He was a gentleman, and liked to think he would have reacted the same way even if she hadn't had sparkling blue eyes and a dimpled chin and such nice curves that not even the plain outfit could disguise them. But those things sure didn't hurt.

"Yes, ma'am, you go right ahead and sit down," said Longarm as he doffed his hat. "I'll be glad for the company. I figured this was going to be a lonely, boring trip."

The woman laughed lightly as she sat. "Well, I hope I can keep you entertained, Mister . . . ?"

"Parker," Longarm said as he lowered himself back to the seat. Might as well keep using the alias, he decided, even if he chucked that hardware salesman nonsense. "Custis Parker."

The woman turned on the seat and extended a gloved hand to him. "I'm Miss Emmaline Colton." Her grip was surprisingly firm as Longarm shook her hand.

"Pleased to meet you, Miss Colton."

"Likewise, Mr. Parker." She took her hand back and asked, "Are you traveling on business?"

"Well . . . not really."

"Then this is a pleasure trip?"

That wasn't strictly true either, thought Longarm. Emmaline Colton was a mite nosy, in addition to being a pretty little thing. Longarm said, "Actually, I'm not sure how things are going to work out. I reckon I'll just have to wait and see when I get there."

"And what is your destination?"

"Trinidad." That was where he would get off the train. From there, a wagon was supposed to pick up passengers bound for Briarcliff Manor and take them out there.

"What a coincidence," Emmaline said. "I'm bound for Trinidad too. Could I ask a favor of you, Mr. Parker?"

Longarm shrugged. "Sure, I guess so. What can I do for you?"

She leaned closer to him, lowering her voice until it was little more than a whisper. "There's a man following me, and I suspect he intends to try to stop me from getting where I'm going. Would you mind terribly killing him for me?"

Chapter 2

Longarm stared at her. He couldn't help the reaction. It wasn't every day that a gal who seemed to be the picture of fresh-faced innocence calmly asked him to murder someone for her.

"Oh, dear," Emmaline said after a moment. "You took me seriously, didn't you?"

"You sounded pretty serious," Longarm told her.

"It's this dreadful sense of humor of mine. As far back as I can remember, I've enjoyed shocking people." She placed a hand on his arm, her touch light, almost like that of a bird. "But I'm telling the truth about one thing, Mr. Parker. A man is following me, and I'm certain he means me no good. Will you help me?"

"Let me get this straight," said Longarm. "You sat down here with me because I looked like I could handle this gent who's causing you trouble, is that it?"

"Well, that certainly helped me make my decision." Emmaline smiled at him. "But I also thought you seemed to be the most handsome, interesting man in the car."

"Well, in that case," Longarm said dryly, "I reckon I *have* to help you. Where can I find the hombre?"

The door at the rear of the car opened, and Emmaline threw a quick glance over her shoulder. Longarm heard her

11

sharply indrawn breath. "Here he comes now," she said in a low voice. "I'm sure he's been searching the cars for me ever since the train left Denver."

Longarm looked back and saw a tall, rawboned man with dark hair, a narrow face, and spectacles. He wore a suit and a bowler hat. He didn't look particularly threatening at first glance, but his shoulders were broad and there was a certain hardness to his jaw. As he started moving up the aisle, he looked from left to right, checking out the passengers on both sides of him. Clearly, he was searching for someone.

According to Emmaline Colton, that someone was her.

Longarm said, "Slide over here next to the window, ma'am." He got to his feet, and as he did so, Emmaline did as he told her, scooting over on the bench seat until she was beside the window, which was lowered a couple of inches. That let in some soot and smoke, but as Longarm moved into the aisle, he was between Emmaline and her pursuer, and that seemed to be the important thing at the moment.

The man glanced in Longarm's direction, then looked past him. His eyes suddenly widened in recognition, and he started forward. Longarm took a step himself, cutting down the gap between him and the man. He rested his hands on the seat backs on either side of him, completely blocking the aisle. The man stopped short; otherwise he would have run into Longarm.

"Hold on there, old son," Longarm said. "What's your hurry?"

"Please, sir, I must get by," the man said politely. He had a slight foreign accent of some kind.

"You're in quite a rush, ain't you?" Longarm leaned forward a little, knowing that would probably force the man to move back. It did.

Skirts rustled behind Longarm. He wondered if Emmaline was making a break for it. She might be, but he didn't turn to look. He kept his eyes fastened on the man in front of him.

"Please," the man said, "I must get by." He was growing more agitated by the second.

"In a minute," said Longarm, "once we've figured out who gets to go first on this here one-way trail."

The man's temper was slipping away from him. *"Ver-dammt Amerikaner,"* he grated. He bulled forward, trying to shoulder past Longarm.

Longarm put a hand in the middle of the man's chest and shoved hard. "I don't savvy your lingo, but I reckon I understood that," he said. "And I don't much cotton to it either."

"You do not understand," the man said. He pointed a shaking finger past Longarm. "She is a thief! And she is getting away!"

Longarm finally glanced over his shoulder and saw that the man was right about one thing: Emmaline Colton was slipping through the door at the front of the car. She threw one frightened look back at the confrontation in the aisle, and then she was gone.

Longarm turned his head back toward the foreigner, just in time to see a knobby-knuckled fist coming right at his face.

His instincts took over, making him duck his head to the side so that the man's fist only grazed his jaw. Still, the blow landed with enough power to stagger Longarm slightly, confirming his guess that the man was more dangerous than he looked. Longarm set his feet and struck while his opponent was slightly off balance, hooking a punch into the man's belly.

The man bent over in pain, but didn't fall. Longarm tried to launch a roundhouse punch at his outthrust chin, but the man lurched forward, going under the blow and tackling Longarm. Longarm went over backward in the aisle.

By this time, the other passengers were shouting questions and curses as the fight broke out in their midst. Longarm ignored them as he grappled with the man. There wasn't much room on the floor of the car between the seats.

13

Longarm had the misfortune to land on the bottom, and the man's weight pinned him down to a certain extent. The man got his hands around Longarm's throat.

The big lawman felt the floor of the car swaying back and forth underneath his head as the train click-clacked over the rails. From this position, he had a view of the man's dark, angry face looming over him, as well as the ceiling of the car. That was about all Longarm could see.

And that was being blotted out by a red haze that dropped over Longarm's eyes as the man's fingers tightened cruelly around his throat.

Longarm brought his right knee up sharply, aiming it at the man's groin. The thrust went home, finding its target with a solid impact that made the man's eyes bug out as if they were about to pop free of their sockets. His mouth opened, and his grip on Longarm's throat loosened. Longarm used both arms to knock the man's hands away, then jabbed a short punch up into his face. The man rocked back, allowing Longarm to heave him off completely.

Gasping for breath, Longarm reached up in an attempt to grab one of the seats and pull himself upright. He latched onto something and hauled himself into a sitting position, but then he saw he hadn't taken hold of one of the seats after all. He was grasping the thigh of the woman who was sitting in the seat, a middle-aged matron who had shrunk back away from the battle, just not quite far enough. She was regarding Longarm with a stare of utter horror.

"Sorry, ma'am," he said quickly as he took his hand off her leg. If his hat hadn't been knocked off already, he would have tipped it to her. As it was, he surged to his feet to confront the foreign man, who was also clambering up from the floor of the aisle.

"Nein," the man said, holding a hand out toward Longarm. He was pale and bent over, his other hand still clutching his balls where Longarm had kneed him.

"Ten," said Longarm, clenching his fists and stepping

forward. He wasn't sure why they were counting, but he was too mad at the moment to really care.

The man shook his head. "No more," he said. "She is gone. We fight for nothing."

Emmaline Colton was gone, that was true enough. But Longarm didn't consider the fracas to be over just yet. "I want you to leave the lady alone," he said. "Just stay away from her."

"But . . . but she steals from me!" the man sputtered.

Longarm's galloping pulse had slowed down a mite, and he thought about what the man was saying. It was true that Emmaline didn't really look like a thief, but in his days as a U.S. deputy marshal, Longarm had run into plenty of pretty gals who were really bank robbers or cattle rustlers or even worse.

"What did she steal?" he asked.

"My skull!"

Now Longarm knew the man was loco. "Your skull?" he repeated.

"It is the greatest archaeological find of the century! And the glory and the fame should have been mine!" The man straightened and shook a fist in anger. "It is the name of Dr. Ulrich Ganz that should have been celebrated all over the world, not that . . . that . . . painted hussy who calls herself a scientist!"

"You mean Miss Emmaline?" asked Longarm with a frown.

"I mean Dr. Colton, though she dishonors the title!"

Well, this was starting to make a little more sense, thought Longarm, although not much. He stepped forward and grasped the man's arm. The man drew back, as if ready to fight again, but Longarm said, "Ease off there, old son. Sit down and tell me about it."

"Why should I?" the man challenged.

Longarm sighed. "Because if you don't, we ain't going to have any choice but to waltz around with fists some more, and I ain't in the mood right now." He pointed to

15

the empty bench where he had been sitting with Emmaline Colton a few minutes earlier. "Now sit, or you'll get sat."

With a glower that his dark, narrow face was perfectly suited for, the man bent over to pick up his hat. Longarm did likewise, keeping a suspicious eye on the man as he did so. Of course, the gent was watching him too. Neither of them was willing to trust the other one.

The man sat down by the window. Longarm brushed off his suit and knocked the dust from his hat, then sat beside the man. "I take it you're Ganz."

The man nodded. "Ulrich Ganz, professor of archaeology and anthropology at the University of Heidelberg."

"Thought you sounded Prussian. And you've got some sort of feud going on with Miss Emmaline?"

"Dr. Colton also teaches in the same field, though at some college for females in your eastern United States." Ganz's voice dripped with contempt. "She fancies herself an archaeologist, but she is a rank amateur."

"Maybe so, but she beat you to something you've been after, didn't she?" guessed Longarm.

Ganz muttered a few words in his native tongue that Longarm figured weren't very complimentary, then went on. "I am sure you have never heard of Neanderthal man."

"Prehistoric hombre, wasn't he?"

Ganz looked surprised. "Yes. The first fossilized remains were found in the valley of the Neander River, near Dusseldorf, about twenty-five years ago. Since then, other archaeological expeditions have found remains in many other locations. Including one in which I was involved in the excavation earlier this year." His voice took on a wistful tone, like that of a man describing a loved one. "We found the most perfect skull, an absolutely beautiful specimen. I dug it out of the dirt myself and cleaned it and . . . and . . . and then she *stole* it!" His words and his expression had turned ugly again.

"Why would a gal steal some old skull?" Longarm wanted to know.

"Because she claims she found it!" snarled Ganz. "True, she was in the pit with me when the specimen came to light, but *I* was the one who unearthed it. It belongs to me."

"What in Hades is she planning to do with it?"

Ganz looked down at his hands, which were clenching and unclenching. "There is an academic conference in your American city of San Francisco next month," he said. "It is my belief that Dr. Colton intends to exhibit the skull there and present a paper claiming that she is responsible for its discovery. I will not allow that, of course."

"You figure to steal it back from her." Longarm's words were a statement, not a question.

Haughtily, Ganz said, "I would merely be reclaiming my property. There is no theft involved."

"Well, the American law might look on that a little differently," said Longarm, without revealing that he himself packed a badge. "Over here we've got a concept known as possession being nine-tenths of the law. Unless you've got a bill of sale or something to prove that the skull belongs to you, which I figure ain't likely."

Ganz laughed harshly. "Of course I have no such documentation."

"Then I reckon you're what we call up the creek without a paddle, old son."

"And just what is your interest in this affair?" Ganz asked with a sneer. "You do not seem to be well acquainted with Dr. Colton."

"Never saw her before today," Longarm admitted. "But she asked for help."

"And you, being an American, had to come to her aid."

"Something like that," snapped Longarm. He didn't much care for the way Ganz had said "American," as if it was a word a fella would say when he was walking across a barnyard and stepped in something. "And if you know what's good for you, you'll leave her alone," Longarm added.

Ganz glared at him. "Still you side with her, even though you now know the truth."

"I know what you say is the truth. I ain't heard her side of it yet."

"She will lie," Ganz said with a dismissive wave of his hand. "She cannot be trusted. She uses her beauty to blind men to the fact that she is a viper."

"That'll be enough of that talk," Longarm said, a hard edge creeping back into his voice.

Ganz stood up. "Let me out of here. I have no wish to continue this pointless conversation."

Longarm got to his feet and moved aside to let Ganz into the aisle. "Go on, and good riddance to you. But remember what I told you. "Leave Miss Emmaline alone."

Ganz just snorted in disgust and stalked toward the back of the car. He went out onto the rear platform and slammed the door behind him.

Longarm was aware that most of the other passengers were looking at him curiously. He didn't blame them. He'd just had a knock-down, drag-out fistfight with Ganz, then sat him down and talked earnestly with him for a spell. Those other folks had to be wondering what was going on.

Longarm grinned and tapped himself on the temple. "Fella was a mite touched in the head," he said by way of explanation. That brought some knowing nods from the other passengers.

Curious as to what had happened to Emmaline Colton, Longarm didn't reclaim his seat. Instead he turned and went forward, leaving the car through the same door through which Emmaline had disappeared a few minutes earlier. He walked across the connecting platforms into the next car and searched among the passengers there for her. Seeing no sign of her, he went on to the next car after that, with the same lack of results.

When he stepped out onto the platform at the front of that car, however, she was there, standing beside the iron railing around the platform. She tensed as Longarm opened the door and emerged from the car, then relaxed a little as she recognized him.

"Mr. Parker!" she exclaimed. "Are you all right? Ulrich didn't hurt you, did he?"

"We just scuffled a mite," Longarm replied, not mentioning how Ganz had tried to choke him to death.

"Where is he now?"

"I sent him on his way. Not before we had a talk, though."

Surprisingly, Emmaline threw back her head and laughed. It was like the sound of a high mountain stream bubbling over rocks. "And I suppose he told you that I stole the Baumhofer Cranium from him."

"Well, he said something about an old skull. . . ."

"*I* found that skull, not Ulrich," Emmaline said. "True, he helped me unearth it, but I was the first one to lay eyes on it, and as such, the right of discovery belongs to me."

Longarm propped a hip against the railing and took a cheroot from his vest. The wind was too strong out here on the platform to allow him to light it, so he settled for chewing on the end as he said, "Ganz claims you're trying to show him up by taking the skull to San Francisco for some sort of scientific conference."

"Archaeologists and anthropologists from all over the world will be there," Emmaline said somewhat breathlessly. "Do you have any idea how much resistance I've encountered over the years to the idea that a woman can be a scientist, Mr. Parker?"

"Quite a bit, I reckon," said Longarm. "And make it Custis."

"All right. I'm Emmaline. You see, Custis, my discovery of the Baumhofer Cranium will finally make the rest of my colleagues take me seriously. It's really a remarkably well-preserved specimen."

If Emmaline had been older, Longarm could've said the same thing about her. As it was, though, she was young and fresh and lovely, and he wondered how she would feel if he tried to steal a kiss. . . .

But he didn't have to, because she said, "And I have you to thank for saving my career, Custis." With that, she stepped toward him and came up on her toes to press her lips to his.

He saw what she was doing in time to get the cheroot out of his mouth, and a second later she was plastered up against him from knees to shoulders, her breasts softly but insistently prodding into his chest as she kissed him. Longarm slid an arm around her waist and pulled her even closer.

She was one hell of a kisser, no doubt about that. Her lips parted and her tongue snaked boldly into Longarm's mouth, darting here and there and exploring with a wet, urgent heat that sent shock waves rumbling all through Longarm. The vibrations came to roost in his pecker, stiffening it until Emmaline had to feel the rock-hard shaft digging into her belly. She didn't pull back and act shocked by his reaction, however. Instead, she just gave a little roll of her hips that lifted her pelvis into a sort of caress of his erect manhood.

Only then did she break the kiss and whisper, "Thank you for helping me, Custis."

Longarm had to swallow a couple of times before he could say, "You're welcome, Miss Emmaline."

She slipped out of his arms and moved a few steps away. His pulse was hammering so hard in his head that he figured it was likely to bust right out through his skull at any moment. Then, in a few thousand years when some future archaeologist dug up his bones, they could look at his skull and wonder what would make a fella's head blow up like that. They could call it the Colorado Cranium.

Well, if nothing else, this whole business with Emmaline Colton and Ulrich Ganz had taken his mind off the job Billy Vail had given him earlier in the day. He glanced around to see where they were. The train had passed Castle Rock and was nearing Pueblo. They'd be in Trinidad by nightfall.

He wasn't ready to take his leave of Emmaline just yet. He cleared his throat and said, "So, you're on your way to San Francisco?"

"Eventually," she replied. "The conference isn't until next month, so I have plenty of time. I thought I'd stop off and visit an acquaintance of mine, perhaps rest up for a week or so before I travel on."

Longarm nodded. "Your friend lives in Trinidad? I recollect you said you were bound for there."

"Outside of Trinidad really, but I'll be leaving the train there. If you're from this area, perhaps you know of him. His name is Sir Alfred Brundage."

Chapter 3

This time, Longarm managed not to gape at her like a damned fool, but he was still mighty shocked and surprised to hear that Emmaline not only knew the man around whom Longarm's current case revolved, but she was also on her way to the same place as Longarm was: Briarcliff Manor.

"He's a brilliant English scientist and physician," Emmaline went on. "I met him a year ago in London, before going on to Prussia for the Baumhofer dig, and when I heard that he had emigrated to America and opened up a health retreat in the Colorado mountains, I knew I had to come visit him. I think some of his mineral bath treatments are exactly what I need to soothe my nerves after the past few months."

Picturing a nude Emmaline sitting in a hot, bubbling mineral bath didn't do much to soothe Longarm's nerves. He tried to put that image out of his mind as he said, "Talk about your coincidences. I'm heading for Sir Alfred's place too."

Emmaline's eyes widened. "Really? That's wonderful, Custis. We'll be able to see each other there and get to know each other better."

After that kiss, Longarm figured they were well on the way to knowing each other pretty intimately. Once they were at Briarcliff Manor, they would have even more opportunities to get close. Of course, he was going there to work, not to play slap-and-tickle with some lovely auburn-haired lady scientist . . . but hell, surely there would be *some* time when he wasn't trying to find out who was trying to kill Sir Alfred or riding herd on Senator Hanley's rambunctious offspring.

"I'll be looking forward to that," he said with a nod. "The getting-to-know-each-other-better part, I mean."

Emmaline smiled. "So will I." She could pack an awful lot of tempting promise in three short words, Longarm discovered.

"What about Ganz?" he asked. "You reckon he'll follow you to Briarcliff Manor and try to bother you again?"

"Try to steal the skull from me, you mean." Emmaline sighed. "Yes, I'd say it's entirely possible he will. But you'll help me watch out for him, won't you, Custis?"

"Damn right I will. He won't pester you anymore if I have anything to say about it."

She put a hand on his arm and squeezed it. "Thank you. You've really turned into my protector, and I barely know you."

"Well, we said we were going to do something about that."

Her smile turned a little devilish. "That's right, we did."

"For now, why don't we go back inside and sit down? I reckon Ganz is probably back in one of the other cars, stewing over things."

"You're probably right. Ulrich has always been quick to brood." Emmaline slipped her arm through Longarm's. "I'll be honored to sit with you, kind sir."

"The honor's all mine, ma'am," Longarm told her.

He was starting to wish Trinidad was farther away, so he'd have more time to spend alone with Miss Emmaline Colton.

•   •   •

The settlement appeared before Longarm was ready for it, a cluster of lights twinkling in the dusk that settled down as the sun disappeared behind the peaks of the Sangre de Cristo range just west of Trinidad. He had thoroughly enjoyed sitting and chatting with Emmaline. She told him about all the various archaeological expeditions she had taken part in, places ranging from Europe to Africa to South America. She had traveled a lot for a woman, and Longarm sort of envied her for that. He had left West-by-God-Virginia after the Late Unpleasantness, and had been down a lot of trails from the Mississippi to the Pacific, from the Milk River to the Rio Grande and beyond, but most of his time had been spent in the western half of the United States. Emmaline had seen the world.

That was why, when she asked him about his own background, he had abandoned the idea of posing as an explorer. Around someone like her, who had really been to such places, his pose would no doubt be revealed as false in a matter of minutes. There was no way he could fool her.

So he fell back on Billy's hardware salesman story, only Longarm made himself the owner of a string of successful hardware stores in Kansas and Nebraska and Missouri. A hardware tycoon, as it were. Someone like that would be able to afford to come to Sir Alfred's health retreat, Longarm figured.

If Emmaline found him dull, she certainly didn't act like it. She laughed at his stories and touched his arm frequently and leaned her shoulder against his as they sat on one of the upholstered benches. When the conductor came through the car, calling, "Trinidad, five minutes! Trinidad, five minutes!" she looked disappointed.

"I was enjoying our talk," she said with a little pout.

"So was I," agreed Longarm, "but since we're going to the same place, there's no reason we can't keep on with it."

That perked her up. "You're right," she said. "I'm supposed to be picked up by a wagon in Trinidad and taken on to Sir Alfred's spa. You too?"

Longarm nodded. "That's what I was told. The wagon's supposed to meet us."

"Then I won't be disappointed that we've gotten here. We shall simply continue our conversation in the wagon."

"How far is it from Trinidad to Briarcliff Manor, do you know?" asked Longarm.

Emmaline shook her head. "Not really. But I got the impression from Sir Alfred's letters that it wasn't too far. Five or ten miles perhaps."

Five or ten miles on mountain roads could take a while, thought Longarm. And it was getting dark too. He hoped the driver of the wagon knew the route well. Narrow trails and hairpin turns could make for some pretty nerve-wracking traveling, especially at night.

The train rolled into the depot on the edge of Trinidad. Since Longarm was working in secret on this case, he had left behind his saddle and his Winchester, and only had a small carpetbag to retrieve from the baggage car. Emmaline wasn't traveling that lightly. A porter hauled out several good-sized bags and piled them on the platform.

Longarm lit a cheroot and then asked Emmaline in a quiet voice, "Where's the, uh, skull? In one of those bags?"

She shook her head. "Oh, no, I wouldn't trust it out of my sight." She lifted the handbag she carried. "I have it in here. Don't worry, it's securely wrapped and padded."

Longarm frowned and pointed with the cheroot at her handbag. "You've got a *human skull* in there?"

"Yes, I just told you I do."

"Wouldn't have thought something like that would fit," Longarm said with a shake of his head.

"Well, Neanderthal man was somewhat smaller than humans are today, and his brain was not as large, so he didn't need as big a brain case. Also, this specimen is smaller than some of the others that have been found, leading me to suspect that it may have belonged to a woman or a child.

What makes it so valuable is its state of preservation, not its size."

Longarm nodded in understanding, but he still cast a wary glance from time to time at Emmaline's handbag. The thought of carrying around a human skull like that made icy fingers tickle along his backbone.

Longarm saw Ulrich Ganz step down from the train at the far end of the platform, and the sight of the Prussian archaeologist made him forget about the skull in Emmaline's handbag for the moment. He kept an eye on Ganz as the man retrieved his baggage. If Ganz even glanced toward them, Longarm couldn't tell. He let himself hope that maybe Ganz had given up on getting the skull back from Emmaline.

But if that was the case, why was Ganz getting off the train? That thought occurred to Longarm and made him frown. He had a feeling they hadn't seen the last of the man.

That hunch turned out to be correct. A few minutes later, a stocky, middle-aged man with a thick mustache came onto the platform from the depot lobby and called out, "Briarcliff Manor! Anybody for the wagon to Briarcliff Manor?"

Longarm lifted a hand, and Emmaline said, "Over here, driver."

As the man came toward them, Longarm spotted Ganz hefting a couple of carpetbags and starting along the platform. Ganz's stride was stiff and determined, and so was the expression on his face.

The driver came up to Longarm and Emmaline and said, "You folks're bound for Briarcliff Manor?"

"That's right," said Emmaline. "I'm Dr. Emmaline Colton. Sir Alfred is expecting me."

"Custis Parker," Longarm introduced himself. "I reckon Sir Alfred knows I'm coming too."

The driver nodded. "Name's Oscar. The wagon's right outside. I'll load your bags."

"I'm traveling light," Longarm said as he lifted the carpetbag, "so I'll give you a hand with the lady's bags."

Oscar glanced at him in surprise. "Ain't often that the guests like to be helpful," he commented.

"Maybe I ain't your ordinary guest," Longarm said with a grin. Oscar didn't know just how true that statement was.

"Driver!"

The harshly spoken word came from Ulrich Ganz, who stalked up to the small group. Oscar turned toward him and said, "What can I do for you?"

"You are the driver to Briarcliff Manor?" demanded Ganz.

"Yep. You bound for there?"

Without answering, Ganz thrust his bags forward, forcing Oscar to take them. "Load these in the wagon," Ganz ordered imperiously.

Oscar wore range clothes and a battered old Stetson, and a revolver rode in a well-worn holster on his hip. His face had been lined and seamed and darkened to the color of old saddle leather by years of exposure to sun and wind and weather. All in all, thought Longarm, not the sort of man to be bossed around by a haughty European son of a bitch like Ganz.

But the fires of anger that flared quickly in Oscar's eyes were just as quickly banked. He nodded and said, "Yes, sir. Wagon's right outside." He might not like taking such abuse, but for some reason, he was prepared to put up with it.

Longarm tucked his own carpetbag under his arm and picked up a couple of Emmaline's bags so that Oscar would have to make only one more trip to get all the baggage loaded. He positioned himself between her and Ganz as they all started through the lobby of the train station, followed by Oscar. The gas lamps in the depot had been lit, giving the place a warm yellow glow.

The wagon parked just outside the long sandstone building had been equipped with three bench seats behind the driver's box. In addition, a canopy had been attached over the seats to provide shade and a measure of protection from the elements. On a warm, breezy evening like this, such protection wasn't really necessary, but Longarm supposed the cover came in handy when it was raining. There was room for the bags behind the rear seat, so he stored them there.

Ganz climbed into the wagon without offering to assist Emmaline. She waited until Longarm gave her a hand to steady her as she stepped up into the vehicle. Ganz had taken the front seat, so Emmaline settled herself onto the rear bench. Longarm joined her.

A moment later, Oscar came hurrying from the station with the rest of the bags. He stowed them behind the seats and them climbed nimbly onto the box and took up the reins. He was about to kick the brake loose and flap the reins at the team of horses hitched to the wagon, when someone shouted, "Sinners!"

The strident cry came from behind them and took Longarm by surprise. He heard Oscar mutter, "Oh, hell." Before Oscar could get the wagon moving, a dark figure had scurried around and placed himself in front of the team.

The figure was dark because it was wearing a black suit and hat, Longarm saw. The man was tall and skinny and holding something in his right hand. He shook it at them, and Longarm realized it was a bible. That and the man's next words confirmed Longarm's guess: The fella blocking their path was some sort of reverend.

"Repent now of your wickedness, while you still have the chance!" he exhorted them. "The Lord shall rain down hellfire and brimstone on the dens of iniquity, and all who partake of their sin shall be destroyed!"

Oscar sighed and said, "Why don't you just get out of the way now, Reverend Jones, 'fore I have to go find the sheriff and cause trouble for you?"

"The only trouble you cause, brother, is for your own

immortal soul by working for that minion of Satan, that demon in earthly guise!"

Longarm leaned forward and asked, "What in blazes is he talking about?"

The preacher heard the question and moved toward the wagon with a quick, crab-like motion. "Blazes is right, brother!" he exclaimed. He didn't seem capable of talking in anything less than a hoarse shout. "Blazes is where you'll wind up if you venture into that house of sin!"

Emmaline said, "Surely you can't be talking about Briarcliff Manor."

Reverend Jones flinched back at the very mention of the place. "Sodom and Gomorrah, you might as well call it! Filled with every manner of vice and perversion known to man!"

"But it's a health spa," Emmaline protested.

Finally, Jones lowered his voice. In a harsh whisper, he said, "That's what Brundage would like you to believe." His voice rose again. "But I know what really goes on there!" He turned and grabbed the team's harness with his free hand. "I'll hold these beasts of Satan! Flee! Flee now while you have the chance!"

"Reverend," Oscar said, "let go o' them horses before I come down there and whale on you."

"Do your worst!" Jones shot back at him. "Do your worst, and be damned to you! 'Yea, though I walk through the valley of the shadow of death, I will fear no evil—' "

"Obadiah!" This was a new voice, sharp and commanding. A man came striding along the street, trailed by a young woman. Longarm saw light from the train station windows reflecting on a badge pinned to the newcomer's vest. The local law, he thought.

The star packer came up to Jones and took his arm. "Alice told me you were on a tear again," he said. "Come on back to the church with me."

"Betrayed!" snapped Jones as he looked wide-eyed at the young woman. "Betrayed by my own flesh and blood!

29

'How sharper than a serpent's tooth, to have a thankless child!' So says the Good Book!"

Longarm chuckled. "Hate to break it to you, old son, but that ain't Scripture. It's from Shakespeare."

Jones ignored Longarm and continued ranting as the local lawman gently but firmly steered him away from the wagon. Oscar said, "Thanks, Sheriff," and got the vehicle rolling as quickly as possible.

"What was that all about?" Longarm asked when they were away from the depot.

Ganz said, "The man was obviously a lunatic." That was his first comment since getting in the wagon.

Oscar shook his head. "I don't reckon Reverend Jones is crazy. A mite peculiar, sure, but he just believes what he believes real strong."

"I don't understand," said Emmaline. "That man objects on a religious basis to what Sir Alfred does at Briarcliff Manor?"

"Yes'm," replied Oscar. "Reverend Jones, he says it's sinful for folks to do the things they do up at Briarcliff."

"What do *you* think?" Longarm asked.

Oscar's shoulders rose and fell in a shrug. "Ain't up to me to decide. I just fetch folks back and forth from the station and sort of take care of the place."

Longarm frowned in thought and rasped a thumbnail along the line of his jaw. "Is the reverend the only one in Trinidad who feels that way?"

Oscar glanced back at Longarm, wondering maybe why the big man was asking so many questions. He said, "The reverend's got his followers. A regular congregation, I reckon you'd call it."

"And he keeps 'em stirred up about Sir Alfred?"

Again the shrug. "He tries."

That was interesting, Longarm thought as he fell silent. Somebody in these parts had a grudge against Sir Alfred Brundage, a grudge potent enough to lead them to cause trouble for the Englishman. From what he had seen so far, it seemed to Longarm that Reverend Obadiah Jones or one of his flock of followers would make a mighty likely suspect. He was looking forward to talking with Sir Alfred and finding out exactly what had happened to lead him to ask for help.

The wagon left Trinidad and headed west on a road that led into the foothills of the Sangre de Cristos. A faint reddish glow in the sky above the peaks was all that remained of the day. Oscar handled the team well, and Longarm's worries about being able to reach their destination in the dark receded somewhat. Likely Sir Alfred wouldn't have trusted Oscar to pick up the guests if he wasn't pretty competent.

The road wound through the foothills and then lifted higher into the mountains. The lights of Trinidad fell down and away behind them. Emmaline looked around them and said, "My, this must be a spectacular view during the daylight. The mountains remind me a bit of the Alps."

Longarm had never seen the Alps, but he had tracked owlhoots all through the Sangre de Cristos. "Their name means Blood of Christ," he said. "Probably because of the reddish color they've got in places."

"I'm glad I came here. I'm looking forward to seeing Sir Alfred again." Her hand reached over and rested for a moment on Longarm's where it lay against his thigh. "And it gave me the opportunity to meet you, Custis."

Longarm wasn't sure, but he thought he heard Ganz snort quietly in disgust.

He didn't care if the Prussian was eavesdropping. He took Emmaline's hand and squeezed it. "I'm glad I met you too, Miss Emmaline."

She laughed lightly. "I suppose I'll have a difficult time breaking you of that habit so that you'll just call me Emmaline. You Southern gentlemen are all alike."

Longarm considered himself much more of a Westerner now than a Southerner, no matter what his origins, and he was about to explain that to her when the wagon rounded

31

a curve and rolled through the mouth of a shallow valley that lay beneath the beetling brows of the peaks above.

"There she is," Oscar called to his passengers. "Briarcliff Manor."

Chapter 4

It was like something out of a painting, with silvery light from the moon and stars washing down over the valley and illuminating the great house that stood in the center of it. With three stories, complete with arches and spires and gabled windows, it was an impressive structure indeed, and Longarm had a hard time believing it had once been a simple ranch house. Sir Alfred Brundage must have spent a great deal of time and money turning the place into what it was now.

"My God," Emmaline said softly. "It looks almost as if it should be sitting on a moor somewhere in Cornwall."

That was in England, Longarm thought. Emmaline was right; Briarcliff Manor was like nothing he had ever seen before in the American West.

"Mighty fancy," he said. Quickly, he studied the layout of the rest of the valley. A creek meandered along roughly through the center of it, watering the meadows where cattle could graze. He saw the long, regular tree lines of an orchard as well. Several plots of what appeared to be cultivated land were probably vegetable gardens. This valley could likely be self-sustaining in a pinch, as long as the creek didn't go dry. And fed as it surely was by springs and melting snow from the mountains, it was unlikely to dry up any time soon. He found himself looking forward to seeing the valley in the daytime.

The house itself was dark for the most part, Longarm noted. In fact, only one window seemed to have a light in it, and that was on the top floor. He was a little surprised to see the place as dark as that. The hour was still fairly early in the evening. Maybe most of the folks who stayed at Briarcliff Manor went to bed with the chickens. How did that old proverb about early to bed and early to rise go again? he asked himself.

The road wound down a gentle slope to the valley floor, then followed the creek toward the house. The wagon was only a couple of hundred yards from Briarcliff Manor when Longarm suddenly spotted movement on the trail in front of them. Something white flashed through the darkness, and Oscar kicked the brake as he hauled back on the reins with both hands and called, "Whoa!" to the team.

The wagon lurched to a halt. Emmaline leaned forward anxiously and asked, "What's wrong?"

"Don't know," said Longarm as he began to rise to his feet, "but I intend to find out."

His keen eyes peered through the darkness, and now he could make out more details about the person approaching them. For one wild second, he thought it was a ghost, what with all that white fabric flapping around. But then he saw that the figure hurrying along the road and casting nervous glances back over her shoulder was a woman. She wore a long, flowing white gown, and she seemed to be looking toward that lone lighted window in the otherwise dark hulk of Briarcliff Manor. The way she was acting, Longarm thought it was a fair assumption that something had frightened her.

The next moment, he saw what it was as another figure lunged out of the shadows of the trees that lined the trail and pounded after the running woman. She let out a scream and tried to increase her speed, but she was no match for the long-legged gait of her pursuer. The shadowy figure swooped down on her, wrapping itself around her like living darkness. The woman's second scream was cut short.

"Mein Gott!" exclaimed Ulrich Ganz, and Emmaline gasped as she held a hand to her mouth in shocked surprise. Only Oscar didn't seem overly startled.

Longarm had an idea there was more going on here than was evident, but he had never been the sort to stand by and watch while a woman was in trouble. He hopped down from the wagon and trotted forward, ignoring Oscar's hurried call of "Wait a minute, Mr. Parker!"

The two figures struggling in silence in the middle of the trail paid no attention to Longarm until he strode up to them, reached out to grab a handful of darkness that turned out to be some sort of cloak, and gave a hard tug on it. "Hey!" he said sharply. "Let go of the lady, mister."

The figures parted, and in the moonlight, Longarm saw that the woman was young and fair-haired and lovely. The neckline of her flowing white gown had been pulled down so that the nipple of her left breast was peeking over it. That breast, like its twin on the right, was firm and good-sized, and both of them were heaving up and down as their owner panted in fear.

The tall man wearing the black cloak turned quickly toward Longarm. The cloak flared out around him. "What the hell!" he said. "Damn it! Who do you think you are?"

Longarm could see the man better now. He was young too, with a thick shock of dark hair and a blousy white shirt and tight black trousers under that black cloak. The shirt was open about halfway down his torso, revealing a muscular, practically hairless chest.

"Who do you think *you* are?" Longarm shot back at the gent.

The man's lip lifted in a sneer. "The man who's about to hand you a sound thrashing!" He swung a fist at Longarm's head.

The woman in white said, "Mark! No!"

Longarm was used to ducking punches, but twice in one

day was too much. He neatly evaded the wildly telegraphed blow, then stepped in and grabbed the man's shoulders. A quick twist spun the man around, and Longarm moved up behind him and looped his left arm around his throat. At the same time, he grabbed the fellow's right arm with his other hand and jerked it behind his back. The man in the cloak wasn't going anywhere, not without dislocating that arm, and he wasn't going to be able to breathe much either, with Longarm's forearm pressed across his throat like an iron bar.

With the immediate threat taken care of, Longarm had time to think about what he had just heard. The woman had called this man "Mark." Longarm knew somebody by that name who was supposed to be on his way to Briarcliff Manor, but it was his understanding that Mark Hanley wasn't supposed to arrive until the next day.

Anyway, hardware store owner Custis Parker wouldn't know anything about a senator's son, so Longarm couldn't very well ask his opponent if he was Mark Hanley. Mentally cursing once more the fact that he was doing this job in secret, Longarm grated, "Settle down there, old son. I don't want to hurt you."

"Let him go, you big bully!" said the woman in white. She rushed at them and started swatting at Longarm, reaching past the hombre called Mark to do so. Longarm ducked his head, unsure what to do next.

Emmaline came to his rescue. She had climbed down from the wagon and hurried forward, and now she grabbed the arm of the woman in white and jerked her away from Longarm. "Stop it!" she said.

The woman in white let out an offended "Oh!" and lunged at Emmaline, grabbing her hair with one hand and knocking her hat askew, while with the other she clawed at the redhead's face. Emmaline knocked that hand aside before the long fingernails could find her eyes and grabbed the woman's wrist, then pivoted with as neat a wrestling move as Longarm had ever seen, sticking out a hip and throwing the woman in white over it. The woman in white landed in the trail with an "Ooofff!" and Emmaline came down on top of her, planting a knee in her midriff and grabbing hold of both her shoulders.

The man Longarm was holding wheezed, "M-Margaret!" He sounded genuinely alarmed, and he started struggling harder against Longarm's hold on him, even though all he succeeded in doing was cutting off even more of his air.

This had gone on just about long enough, thought Longarm. He looked toward the wagon, where Oscar was sitting on the driver's seat, sadly shaking his head. Behind him, Ganz was laughing at the spectacle in the road.

"Oscar," said Longarm, "do you know these folks?"

"I'm afraid so, Mr. Parker," the driver replied. "They're guests here. The gent you're hanging onto is Mr. Mark Hanley, and the lady on the ground there is Lady Margaret Wingate."

"Oh!" exclaimed Emmaline. She'd had no idea she was manhandling British nobility. She let go of the woman in white and stood up, saying, "I beg your pardon, Lady Margaret. I think this whole thing must be a dreadful misunderstanding."

Lady Margaret sat up, either not knowing or not caring that her entire left breast had escaped the confines of the gown now. She said coldly, "Yes. A misunderstanding."

Longarm wasn't ready to let go of the gent he was holding. Not until Mark Hanley was clear on a couple of matters. "No more throwing punches at me," Longarm said. "And don't go grabbing ladies neither."

Hanley's head jerked up and down in a weak nod. He was probably getting pretty short of breath by now. Longarm released him and stepped back, and Hanley gulped down several lungfuls of air as he lifted a hand and rubbed his bruised throat. He glared at Longarm and rasped, "You buffoonish bastard!"

"I didn't say anything about name-calling," Longarm

drawled, "so I'll let it go this time. Just don't try it again, old son."

Lady Margaret got to her feet, finally glanced down at her bare breast, and casually tucked it back into the gown. "Oscar," she said, "who are these . . . these barbarians?"

"More guests of Sir Alfred's, Lady Margaret," Oscar said. "I don't reckon they meant any harm."

"We certainly didn't," put in Emmaline. "It's just that we saw you fleeing from something—or someone—apparently in fear of your life, and then this man attacked you—"

"We were enacting a scene from *Varney the Vampyre*." Lady Margaret said with a sniff.

Longarm recognized the title as being that of a famous "penny dreadful" novel that had also been adapted into a widely performed stage play. He said, "So you weren't really scared at all?"

"Certainly not," said Lady Margaret.

That meant she hadn't been panting in fear, thought Longarm. Lust was more likely. He'd heard of folks play-acting like that before they got around to their romping. They claimed it spiced things up and made it more interesting. Longarm had always found bedding a desirable gal to be plenty interesting all by itself, but he supposed what other folks did was their own business.

"Sorry," he said curtly to Mark Hanley. "We didn't mean to interfere."

Hanley wasn't going to be a good sport about it. "Next time think before you go rushing in like an ignorant lout."

"Now, Mark," Lady Margaret said as she moved closer to Longarm, "the gentleman has apologized for the misunderstanding. What more can we expect from him?"

The way her eyes were now roaming boldly over Longarm, he thought maybe Lady Margaret really was expecting something else from him. Just not here and now, but later, when they could be alone.

Emmaline said, "I apologize too, Lady Margaret, Mr. Hanley. We meant no harm."

Hanley smiled for the first time. "No harm done, I suppose, my dear," he said to Emmaline. He took a half-step that brought him closer to her.

Longarm expected Lady Margaret to react jealously to the attention that Hanley was paying to Emmaline. Instead she turned to the redhead and said with a smile, "Don't trouble yourself, darling." Her hand came up and touched Emmaline lightly on the cheek, a brushing motion that was almost a caress. "You're a very . . . assertive . . . young woman, aren't you?"

Oscar flapped the reins and called out to the team, sending the wagon rolling forward. "Why don't all you folks climb aboard, and we'll go on to the manor?" he suggested.

Emmaline looked grateful for that. She slipped out from between Hanley and Lady Margaret and stepped over quickly to join Longarm. She linked her arm with his and said, "Yes, let's go on."

Oscar brought the wagon to a stop beside the four of them. Longarm helped Emmaline up into one of the empty seats while Hanley assisted Lady Margaret into the other. Longarm couldn't be sure because of the moonlight, but he thought Emmaline was blushing furiously.

The wagon rolled on toward the big house, and a few moments later it came to a stop in front of Briarcliff Manor. Someone inside must have been watching for the arrival of the new guests, because one of the massive double doors at the entrance swung open, and a man stepped out holding an ornate golden candlestick with a candle in it. The glow from the candle revealed the man to be rather small and mild-looking, with wispy fair hair above kindly features. "Good evening, my friends," he said in a cultured British accent, "and welcome to Briarcliff Man—" He stopped short and frowned as he spotted Lady Margaret and Mark Hanley in the wagon along with Longarm, Emmaline, and Ulrich Ganz. "Lady Margaret! Mr. Hanley!" he exclaimed. "What are you—oh! Oh, dear. Pardon my indiscretion."

Hanley swung down from the wagon. "Think nothing of

it, old man," he said, then turned back to help Lady Margaret step from the vehicle.

"Yes, Sir Alfred, there was no real harm done," Lady Margaret assured the man with the candle, who was obviously Sir Alfred Brundage. "But if you will excuse me, I believe I will go ahead and retire for the evening."

Longarm thought Hanley looked disappointed for a second, until Lady Margaret cast a quick, meaningful glance in his direction. Longarm would've been willing to bet that Hanley would be knocking discreetly on the door of Lady Margaret's room less than ten minutes after the lady had "retired for the evening."

"Of course, my dear," Brundage assured her.

"I'll turn in too," Hanley said gruffly, though Longarm didn't know who the young man thought he was fooling.

The two of them went into the house, leaving Sir Alfred to turn toward his new guests. His eyes widened in recognition and a smile appeared on his face as Longarm helped Emmaline down from the wagon. "Emmaline!" Sir Alfred said happily. "You made it. I'm so glad to see you again."

Once she was on her feet, Emmaline stepped forward and embraced her host. "I'm glad to see you again too, Sir Alfred," she said. "Thank you for inviting me to visit you."

"We don't have to worry about titles, my dear," he told her. "I'm just Alfred to my friends and colleagues." He turned to Longarm. "And you, sir, are . . . ?"

"Custis Parker," Longarm said, sticking out his hand. Brundage shook it, though with a bit of reluctance. "You've been expecting me, I reckon," Longarm went on. "I'm in hardware, from the Midwest."

"Ah. I see." That hardware reference should have been enough to tell Brundage who Longarm really was. Evidently it was, because he went on. "I have indeed been expecting you, sir, and I'm quite glad to see you here at last."

Brundage sounded relieved, all right, thought Longarm.

He wondered if anything else suspicious had happened recently. As soon as possible, he needed to catch a moment or two alone with Brundage so he could get the lay of the land.

Ganz had climbed down from the wagon, and he stepped forward now, not caring if he interrupted anything. "I am Dr. Ulrich Ganz," he announced coldly. "I am sure my name is familiar to you, Sir Alfred."

Brundage frowned. "Of course I have heard of you, Dr. Ganz. But I don't believe I was expecting you to be one of my guests."

"I am here because of *her*." Ganz jerked a thumb at Emmaline.

"He's trying to steal something from me, Alfred," Emmaline said quickly. "Can't you send him away?"

Brundage's frown deepened. "Is this true, Dr. Ganz?"

Ganz's lips drew back from his teeth in an angry grimace. "The only thief here is Dr. Colton. She has robbed me of one of the greatest archaeological finds of the century—"

"That's not true!" Emmaline protested. "The Baumhofer Cranium is mine."

"Enough," said Brundage, holding up a hand. "Dr. Ganz, I am well known for my hospitality, so I will not insist that you leave tonight. However, since Dr. Colton was invited to Briarcliff Manor and you were not, I would appreciate it a great deal if you would return to Trinidad in the morning and go on about your business elsewhere."

"My business is here," said Ganz, his voice practically a snarl. He reached inside his coat, and Longarm tensed a little. All Ganz was after was a wad of cash, however. "I can pay for my stay. This is a health retreat, *ja*? My health is in need of your treatments."

Brundage shook his head firmly. "This is a private institution, Dr. Ganz. You cannot simply buy your way in. I repeat, you can stay the night, but in the morning you must leave."

Ganz muttered a few Germanic curses, but finally nodded

in agreement. Brundage turned to the wagon and said, "Oscar, if you'll bring in the bags, I'll show our new guests around." He smiled at Longarm and Emmaline. "Not the full tour, of course. That will have to wait until morning. But I'll show you to your rooms and point out a few things along the way." He offered his arm to Emmaline. "My dear?"

She took it, leaving Longarm to trail along behind the two of them. Ganz came along too, Longarm noted. He kept an eye on the Prussian because Ganz was still eyeing Emmaline's handbag. Longarm suppressed another small shudder as he thought about what she was carrying in there.

Brundage led them through a luxuriously appointed foyer and into a long, high-ceilinged hall. "All our meals are served here," he said. "The food is prepared with the health and well-being of the guests in mind, and we ask that during your stay here, you eat nothing except what is prepared in our kitchen."

"Hope the grub's good," said Longarm.

"Oh, it's quite tasty," Brundage assured him. "But you might find the fare a bit different from your normal diet."

Longarm wondered what he meant by that, but Brundage didn't offer any explanation. Instead, he took them through the dining room and into a corridor lined with small cubicles on both sides. "These are the massage rooms. I've discovered that a vigorous massage before dining stimulates the digestive system." The group turned a corner into another corridor. "These are cleansing rooms, for those whose systems need purging."

Longarm didn't care much for the sound of that, but he didn't say anything. He figured his insides were already as clean as regular doses of good old-fashioned Maryland rye could make them. Just because he was pretending to be one of Sir Alfred's "patients" didn't mean he had to go through with the whole rigmarole.

The path led out through French doors into a garden. Several pools shone in the moonlight, and tendrils of steam rose from them. "The mineral baths," Brundage said. "The centerpiece of our treatment regimen."

"How many guests do you have at the moment?" asked Emmaline.

"Approximately two dozen," Brundage replied. "That's normally our limit, but we're a bit over right now because Mr. Hanley arrived a few days earlier than I expected. He was quite anxious to get here, having heard such wonderful things about Briarcliff Manor."

That explained why Hanley was already here, thought Longarm. Well, this way he wouldn't have to wait for the troublesome youngster to show up.

Brundage led them to a broad outside staircase that curved up to a balcony on the second floor at the rear of the mansion. "The sleeping quarters are up here," he said. "You'll find your rooms quite comfortable, I hope." He glanced at Ganz. "Unfortunately, Doctor, I won't be able to offer you one of the normal guest rooms. But there is a storage area where Oscar can set up a cot."

"That will be satisfactory," Ganz said coldly.

"Are there locks on the doors?" asked Longarm. He wouldn't put it past Ganz to start sneaking around in the dark in an effort to get his hands on that Neanderthal skull in Emmaline's bag.

"Locks?" Brundage said with a small laugh. "No, I'm afraid not, Mr. Parker. Everyone here is open and honest with each other. Such an atmosphere of trust is vital to the treatment. My aim is to heal not only the body but the spirit as well. I trust that meets with your approval?"

Longarm shrugged. He'd slept with a gun in his hand before; he supposed he could do it again. But if somebody was trying to kill *him,* as Brundage claimed was the case here, Longarm sure would have had some locks put on the doors.

"What's on the third floor?" Emmaline asked.

"That's our special cleansing area, used only under certain circumstances."

43

Longarm wondered what Brundage meant by that. He wondered as well when he would have a chance to have a long talk with the Englishman. He hoped it would be soon.

"Here we are," Brundage said as he led them into the second-floor corridor. "Your room, my dear." He stopped with Emmaline in front of one of the doors. "And you'll be directly across the hall, Mr. Parker."

"Excellent," murmured Emmaline. "I'll sleep better knowing that you're nearby, Custis."

"Yeah," said Longarm, with a hard stare directed at Ganz. "That way nobody'll bother you."

Brundage opened the door of Emmaline's room. "Your bags have already been brought up. I shall bid you good night and look forward to seeing you in the morning, bright and early."

"Yes." Emmaline clutched Brundage's hands for a second. "Thank you again, Alfred, for inviting me."

"My pleasure, my dear." He turned to Longarm. "Good night, Mr. Parker."

Longarm nodded. " 'Night."

"Come along, Dr. Ganz." Brundage took the Prussian on down the hall and around a corner, but as he disappeared, Ganz cast one glowering glance back at Longarm and Emmaline, who still stood in the corridor in front of their respective doors.

When Brundage and Ganz were gone, Emmaline said, "Well, I suppose this is good night, Custis."

The corridor was lit by a single lamp in a wall sconce on either end, and Longarm thought Emmaline looked lovely in the soft glow. He remembered the way she had kissed him on the train, how her hips had moved against him and how the softness of her belly had pressed into the rigid spike of his manhood. The memory made him start to harden again, so he forced it out of his mind. He was here to do a job, and he didn't want to get distracted even before he'd had a chance to talk things over with Sir Alfred.

He lifted a hand and tugged on the brim of his Stetson. "Good night, ma'am."

Emmaline laughed. "Back to the Southern gentleman, I see."

"I reckon," said Longarm with a shrug.

Emmaline stepped closer to him and came up on her toes, brushing a quick kiss across his lips. "We'll see about that," she murmured, then turned and was gone, vanishing into her room as the door closed softly behind her.

Longarm gave a long sigh and a little shake of his head, then turned to go into his own room.

He hadn't quite made it when he heard the sharp cry from somewhere down the corridor.

Chapter 5

The sound wasn't very loud to start with, and it was muffled behind one of the doors to boot. But it was distinct enough to stop Longarm in his tracks. It sounded like somebody in one of these rooms was in pain. He started down the hall, moving with a silent grace surprising in such a big man.

He paused before the first door he came to, his eyes widening as he heard a groan from the other side of the panel. Longarm leaned closer, practically putting his ear against the door. He wasn't sure if this was the room from which the first cry had come, but he figured it was a pretty safe bet. He heard another moan. . . .

But no one in there was in pain, he realized, because interspersed with the moans and groans was another sound that was familiar to him:The telltalesqueaking of bedsprings.

Longarm grimaced. He'd nearly made a potentially embarrassing mistake. Nobody was being murdered after all. The sounds had been cries of passion.

A yelp suddenly came from behind the door across the corridor.

Longarm's grimace turned into a frown. He slipped across the hall and listened at that door. Sure enough, folks were going at it in there too. There was no mistaking the sound of bedsprings punctuated by panting breaths and little cries. Longarm shook his head. First Hanley and Lady Margaret had been playing their lusty game outside, and now it appeared that a lot of the same thing was going on in the manor's guest rooms. At least Longarm understood now why the place was mostly dark despite the early hours. Folks had already gotten down to business.

Curiosity compelled him to check some of the other doors. Feeling a little like a Peeping Tom as he did so, he found that amorous activity was going on behind more than half of them. The place sounded more like a whorehouse than a health retreat, he thought. But on the other hand, he supposed, what could be healthier than a lot of hot, sweaty lovemaking?

He walked quickly back to the door of his own room, not wanting anyone to come along and catch him eavesdropping on other folks having their fun. He turned the knob and stepped inside. Habit made him take a fast step to the side, something he always did when entering a strange room. His hand was on the butt of the double-barreled derringer attached to the end of his watch chain. The little gun rode in one vest pocket, serving as a fob for the watch in the other pocket. It was also the only gun Longarm was carrying at the moment; his .44 in its normal cross-draw holster was stashed away in his carpetbag, since it wasn't very likely that a hardware tycoon would be openly packing iron in a gunfighter's rig.

The room was empty except for a comfortable-looking four-poster bed, a dressing table, a wardrobe, a straight chair, and an upholstered armchair. A thick rug was on the floor. In the light from the corridor, Longarm saw a lamp on the dressing table. He lit it and shut the door, then glanced at the window. Thick velvet curtains were draped over it. No one could spy on him very easily.

The door might not have a lock, but the room had a chair, and Longarm didn't waste any time in wedging its back under the knob. He saw his carpetbag on the bed where Oscar had left it. A quick glance in the bag told Longarm that it had not been searched. All his customary telltales were still in place.

He tossed his Stetson on the dressing table and started stripping off his clothes. The day had been long, and he was tired. He peeled his duds down to the bottoms of his long underwear, then stretched out on the bed, which was every bit as soft and comfortable as it looked. He laced his fingers together behind his head and stared up at the ceiling, thinking about everything he had seen and heard since arriving in Trinidad.

Judging by the behavior of Hanley and Lady Margaret, as well as what he had heard going on behind the closed doors of the guest rooms, Briarcliff Manor was a pretty lusty place. For all Longarm knew, that could be part of Sir Alfred's treatment. It went a ways toward explaining why the Reverend Obadiah Jones there in Trinidad had been carrying on the way he had. The reverend had called Briarcliff Manor a den of iniquity. Did he know about what really went on up here? It seemed likely he did, Longarm decided. But would he be incensed enough about it to try to kill Brundage?

Wouldn't be the first time somebody had tried to commit murder in the name of holiness, reflected Longarm.

Before he could get any further in his thinking, a soft knock came from the door. Longarm sat up sharply. His hand reached out instinctively and closed over the derringer, which he had placed on a little table beside the bed. He picked the weapon up as he swung his feet to the floor.

Padding silently on bare feet, Longarm went to the door and stood on one side of it. "Who is it?" he called, holding the derringer ready. He halfway expected he knew what the answer would be, but he hadn't lived this long by taking foolish chances.

"It's me, Custis. Emmaline Colton."

A grin tugged at Longarm's mouth. He had been right.

But he was still cautious, so he asked, "You alone?"

"Of course."

Longarm had no reason to disbelieve her. He tucked the derringer into the waistband of his underwear at the small of his back and then moved the chair out of the way. He opened the door.

Emmaline asked, "May I come in?"

Longarm almost couldn't speak, so overwhelmed was he by her beauty. She was wearing a green silk robe, and her hair was loose around her shoulders. The robe was belted tightly around her trim waist, but the top of it gaped open enough for him to see the beginnings of the creamy valley between her breasts. Longarm found his tongue after a second and said, "Sure, come on in." He stepped back to usher her into the room.

The silk robe swished around her legs as she came in. Longarm closed the door behind her, then turned to watch her. She smiled at him and said, "I'm sure you're shocked at how bold I'm being."

Longarm shook his head. "Not too shocked. Maybe pleasantly surprised would be a better way of putting it."

"At least it's not an unpleasant surprise."

"Nope. Not hardly."

She moved a step closer to him. "Custis, I was wondering . . . you must know about some of the theories Sir Alfred espouses, or else you wouldn't be here."

"If you're talking about all the slap-and-tickle that's going on around here, I'm starting to figure it out," said Longarm.

"Sir Alfred believes in an open and honest expression of one's sexual desires, believes that freely indulging them has a cleansing effect not only on the body but on the soul and the mind as well."

"So folks come here to do pretty much whatever they want, and nobody disapproves?"

Emmaline smiled. "Exactly. And it's equally fine if

someone *doesn't* want to participate. One choice is just as valid as the other."

"But that's not what *you've* decided," said Longarm.

Emmaline's smile grew more sultry. "Not at all. I believe in free expression too." Her hands went to the belt around her waist and untied it with a quick motion. The robe spread open, revealing what Longarm had suspected from the first: She was nude underneath it.

She shrugged off the robe and let it fall to the floor around her feet, then stood there with her eyes half-closed and seemed to revel in the way Longarm's eyes explored her body. Her skin was fair, almost milky, and dotted here and there with freckles. Her breasts were not overly large, but they were firm and rode proudly on her rib cage. The nipples were dark pink and hardening under Longarm's gaze. From there his eyes played down over her flat belly to the slight mound between her thighs that was covered with thick, dark-red hair. Her legs were equally lovely, long and muscular from the treks she had made all over the world. She turned slowly as he watched, giving him a long, loving look at the rear view as well. As she bent over to pick up her fallen robe, Longarm's pulse began hammering in his head once again. He stepped forward, his shaft hard as steel, a growl rising in his throat.

Emmaline tossed the robe on the bed and turned to meet him. She came into his arms, her breasts flattening against his muscular, hairy chest. His mouth dropped onto hers, and her lips opened without hesitation, allowing him to plunge his tongue into her mouth. He buried one hand in her thick hair, while the other slid down her back to cup her bottom and pull her more tightly against him.

The kiss had both of them breathless by the time they broke it. Emmaline moved back just enough so that she could kneel in front of him. Her hands dug under the waistband of his underwear and started to pull it down. Longarm reached behind him and snagged the derringer, palming it and tossing it behind the pillow on the bed. Emmaline didn't seem to notice. She was too busy freeing his manhood from the prison that confined it. As she tugged the underwear down, his shaft sprang free, bobbing up and nearly hitting her in the eye.

"Oh, my," she breathed. "That thing's a deadly weapon, isn't it?"

"Nobody's ever died from it yet," Longarm told her.

"I think I'd like to try," she said as she finished pulling down his underwear. It was bunched around his ankles, but Longarm didn't have a chance to step out of it. It was all he could do to stay standing as Emmaline leaned forward, her mouth open, and engulfed the head of his shaft.

Not surprisingly for such a world traveler, she was damned fluent in French, Longarm discovered over the next few minutes. She took her time, the tip of her tongue teasing his little slit for a moment before it began moving in heated circles. Gradually, she worked her way down, swallowing more and more of him. She couldn't take it all, of course, but she had more than half of the thick, fleshy pole in her mouth before she was through. She reached behind him with one hand and dug her fingers into the cleft between his buttocks, while with the other she cupped and caressed the heavy sacs between his legs.

Longarm was trembling from the sensations she sent coursing through him. He didn't want to spend his climax in her mouth unless that was what she really wanted, so he tugged on her shoulders. "Better ease off," he warned her.

She did so, causing a keen sense of loss to go through him as her mouth released him. But then he was distracted by the way she lay back on the bed and spread her legs. "Now me, Custis," she said breathlessly. "Please."

Longarm was glad to oblige. He dropped to his knees beside the bed and cupped his hands under her bottom, pulling her closer to him as he leaned forward. The lips of her femininity were already covered with dew. His tongue slid along them, lapping at her moisture and spreading her open even more. Emmaline's fingers tangled in his hair as she arched herself against his lips and his probing tongue. He nipped at her little bud of flesh with his teeth, and her thighs tightened around his ears as she began to pant harshly and pump her hips back and forth. A fella could suffocate like this, Longarm thought fleetingly, but he supposed there were worse ways to go.

Finally, a series of deep shudders went through Emmaline, shaking her to her core. She fell back on the bed, as every muscle in her body seemed to go limp. Longarm moved over her, knowing that he could not wait any longer. He drove into her, sheathing himself with such intensity that both of them slid halfway across the bed. Emmaline would have screamed if Longarm had not kissed her at the same moment he was filling her to the brim.

He knew a sense of satisfaction as he felt her plunge directly from the pinnacle of one climax into another, and then another. She was spasming around him so urgently that he had no chance of holding back. He was able to thrust only half a dozen times before his own culmination boiled up from inside him. He gave one final lunge, burying himself within her as deeply as he could possibly go, and then began emptying himself into her. His seed shot out, spurt after scalding spurt, and Emmaline shook and clutched at him and bucked crazily underneath him. Longarm's climax seemed to go on forever.

But it finally ended, plunging him back to earth. He rolled to the side, taking his weight off Emmaline, who was having as much trouble catching her breath as Longarm was. When he could speak again, he said, "Well, I don't know about you . . . but I reckon I feel cleansed, all right."

Emmaline curled against him, laughing. "Oh, Custis," she managed to say, "I'm so glad I met you."

Longarm put his arm around her, and they lay there that way for several minutes, sated and contented, until Longarm suddenly heard a faint noise from out in the hall. He frowned as he lifted his head. He would have sworn what he'd heard had been a door either opening or closing.

"That skull of yours," he said, "where is it?"

"Oh, my God!" Emmaline cried softly as she jerked up-right. "I left it in my room. I was so . . . I was thinking about you . . . I forgot . . ."

Longarm bit back a curse as he swung his legs out of bed. He reached behind the pillow and picked up the der-ringer that was still lying where he had tossed it. Emmaline gasped in surprise when she saw the little gun. Longarm regretted having her discover that there had been a loaded gun in bed with them the whole time, but he was damned if he was going to let Ganz get away with stealing that skull. Emmaline wouldn't have forgotten and left it over there in her room if she hadn't been so hot and bothered by the prospect of paying a visit to Longarm. That might not be very modest, he thought fleetingly, but it was the truth.

He didn't take the time to pull on his long underwear. He just stalked across the room and yanked the door open.

Lady Margaret Wingate exclaimed, "Oh!"

She was standing in front of Emmaline's door, still wear-ing the white gown she'd had on earlier, but now she also wore a filmy pink wrap over it. As she turned to face Long-arm, her eyes dropped immediately to his groin, taking in the length and heft of his organ, which, even in its currently flaccid state, was impressive. Despite the fact that he had just climaxed with Emmaline, Longarm felt a slight stiff-ening in his shaft as Lady Margaret stared at it.

Longarm retreated behind the partially open door, leav-ing Lady Margaret with a slight look of disappointment on her face. She said, "You startled me, Mr. Parker."

"Thought I heard something out here in the hall," said Longarm, "like somebody snooping around."

"It was just me, I'm afraid. I was looking for Dr. Col-ton."

Longarm managed not to glance over his shoulder. He didn't want to give away the fact that Emmaline was here in his room with him. "She's not in her room?"

"No. I opened the door and took a peek."

"Why are you looking for her, if you don't mind my asking?"

"Not at all," Lady Margaret replied with a smile. "I just thought we might engage in a little . . . girl talk."

Longarm wasn't quite sure what she meant by that, nor was he certain that he wanted to know. Instead he said, "I reckon she must be around somewhere. Maybe she went down the hall to the, ah . . ."

"Of course. I'll speak to her another time." Lady Margaret's smile took on a more intimate look as she added, "It was certainly nice seeing *you* again, Mr. Parker. You're quite the . . . gentleman. Good night." She turned and went on her way down the hall, her hips swaying slightly with a natural sensuousness.

Longarm eased the door of his room shut and turned to face Emmaline, who had gotten out of bed and pulled on her robe. The belt was tied around her waist again, and this time the top of the robe was firmly closed.

"False alarm," Longarm told her. "It was just Lady Margaret, not Ganz."

"What did Lady Margaret want with—" Emmaline stopped short and raised a hand. "No, don't answer that. What's important is that no one has tampered with the Baumhofer Cranium. I have to check and make sure it's all right."

Longarm stepped back and opened the door again. Emmaline hurried out and went across the hall to her room. While she was gone, Longarm pulled on his underwear and the trousers from his brown tweed suit. He slipped the derringer into the pocket of the trousers and went out barefooted into the hall. Emmaline had left her door open a few inches, so Longarm didn't hesitate to open it more and step into her room.

"Is it all right?" he asked her. She was standing near the bed with a paper-wrapped object in her hand. Her handbag lay open on the bed.

"I'll know in a moment," she replied as she began stripping away the paper.

Longarm wanted to look away, but his fascination wouldn't allow him to do so. He watched as Emmaline unwrapped the prehistoric artifact. Longarm had seen several human skulls before, and he would have had no trouble recognizing that the object cradled so carefully in Emmaline's hands was one. It was small, though, as she had said, and something about the shape of it struck Longarm as a little odd. It was that ridge above the eye sockets, he realized after a moment, and the way the forehead sloped back sharply. He remembered from his reading in the library that Neanderthal man was considered a step up the ladder of evolution as that British scientist Darwin had theorized, but that didn't mean the fella was as smart or had as big a brain as his modern-day counterparts.

"Beautiful, isn't it?" asked Emmaline as she held up the skull.

Longarm wouldn't have gone that far, but he supposed it was pretty impressive to an archaeologist. The skull seemed to be complete, right down to the jawbone, and there were even a few rudimentary teeth still clinging to it. Longarm suppressed a shudder as he thought about how once that hunk of bone had been a vital part of a living, breathing, feeling creature. The brain in that skull had experienced hate and fear and maybe even love, and the eyes in those sockets had looked out on sunrises and sunsets and everything in between. Now it was nothing but a treasure for a couple of scientists to squabble over. Longarm looked away, swallowing the bad taste that unexpectedly rose in his throat.

"Glad that wasn't Ganz skulking around," he said. "I reckon I'd better get back to my room—"

"Oh, no," said Emmaline. "Not before you tell me why you're carrying around a gun."

Longarm had been afraid she'd get back to that. Deciding it would be better not to be defensive about it, he said, "I'd be a damned fool not to. This can still be a rough country out here, and I'm used to carrying quite a bit of money at times, in my business."

"Then you never travel without being armed?"

"Nope," Longarm answered honestly.

"Good," Emmaline said, surprising him. "I suspect that Ulrich carries a weapon at all times too."

Longarm frowned. "I thought he was a professor."

"He is, but he's also a Prussian. They're a warlike people. And despite his academic background, I think that Ulrich sometimes fancies himself to be an ancient Teutonic warrior-knight, like something out of Wagner."

Longarm only vaguely knew what she was talking about, but he nodded anyway. "I reckon I'll see you in the morning," he said. "If I were you, I'd take that chair and wedge the back of it under the doorknob. It's the next best thing to a lock."

"That's exactly what I intend to do." She had finished rewrapping the skull in the paper, and now she slipped it back into her handbag. Then she came over to Longarm and lifted her face for a quick kiss. "What we did earlier was wonderful," she breathed.

"It won't be the last time," Longarm promised her.

"No. It won't."

Her breasts were soft against his chest, and his senses were full of the smell and taste and feel of her. A few more minutes, thought Longarm, and they'd likely be going at it again, only on her four-poster bed this time instead of his. As pleasurable as that prospect was, Longarm knew he had to get some sleep. He was here to catch a would-be killer, after all, and a fella needed to have his wits about him to do that.

He brushed his lips across hers again, then said, "Good night." He was out of the room and back across the hall into his own before she could stop him.

But even so, it was a long time before he dozed off that night. . . .

Chapter 6

The long day, the eventful evening, and the preoccupation that kept him awake until the wee hours left Longarm feeling somewhat weary when he arose the next morning. He washed his face and shaved, put on a fresh shirt and his suit, and felt a little better by the time he came downstairs and entered the big dining room.

Breakfast was in full swing, he found. More than a dozen people were seated at the long hardwood table. They were equally divided between men and women, noted Longarm, and everyone had the cheerful, happy glow of people who had spent the night making love, even a couple who had to be in their sixties. Lady Margaret and Mark Hanley were there, cooing at each other, but Longarm didn't see any sign of Emmaline Colton or Ulrich Ganz. He wondered if he should have checked on Emmaline before he came downstairs. He had listened briefly at her door but had not heard any noises in her room, so he had expected to find her down here already.

Sir Alfred Brundage was seated at the head of the table. He greeted Longarm with a smile and said heartily, "Ah, good morning, Mr. Parker. Please join us."

"Don't mind if I do," said Longarm as he headed toward one of the empty chairs at the table. "I'm more'n ready for a pot of coffee and a stack of flapjacks, maybe with a pile of fried potatoes and some bacon and sausage on the side."

Sir Alfred's eyes widened in horror as he shook his head from side to side. "Oh, my, no. Those things are terrible for you, Mr. Parker. We eat and drink only healthy things here at Briarcliff Manor." He gestured at a pitcher full of some greenish concoction near his elbow. "I'd be glad to pour you a cup of pressed vegetable essence."

Longarm frowned. "No coffee?"

"I'm afraid not."

One of the other men at the table said to Longarm, "Don't worry about it, sir. In a few days, you won't even miss that awful brew."

The woman beside him added, "Yes, once your body has been cleansed, you won't believe you ever drank such things."

"Well, I don't know," Longarm said dubiously as he eyed the pitcher of green liquid. "I reckon I can give it a try. What about the flapjacks and bacon and sausage?"

"We don't partake of meat here at Briarcliff," said Sir Alfred. "But we have fresh fruit and vegetables and all the rice you'd like."

"Rice?" said Longarm.

"Yes, it's the most healthful grain. The Chinese live on a diet of rice and vegetables and a little fish, you know, and they live long, healthy lives."

Longarm frowned. Billy Vail hadn't said a damned thing about having to eat like a Chinaman when he'd given Longarm this job.

"I'll give it a try," he said with a sigh.

"Good. Because that's really your only option if you want to stay here, you know." Brundage poured a cup full of thick green liquid from the pitcher and slid it over to Longarm. "You'll see, Mr. Parker. A few days of this fare, and you'll feel like a new man."

Yeah, a man who's starving to death for real food, thought Longarm as he picked up the cup. He sniffed the contents, then took a sip. His eyes narrowed and his jaw tried to lock up on him, but he managed to swallow the stuff.

"Wonderful, isn't it?" asked Brundage, beaming.

"Yeah," Longarm choked out. "Wonderful."

He nursed the cup of evil-tasting liquid for a few minutes until a woman in a cook's apron appeared and placed a bowl of some sort of mush in front of him. It didn't look and smell quite as bad as the green stuff, and when Longarm tried it cautiously, he found that it didn't taste too bad either. Sort of bland, but he could stand it.

He didn't join in the happy, chattering conversation going on around him. He was still worried about Emmaline, but that worry was eased a few minutes later when she appeared in the entrance to the dining room, carrying her handbag. She looked fresh and pretty in a blue dress dotted with little yellow flowers. Obviously, she had slept well the night before, and Longarm took a little bit of pride in that fact.

There was an empty chair beside him. Emmaline came over and sat down, casting a sideways glance at him and smiling. A blush started to spread over her face. It should have been clear to anyone who looked at her what she was thinking about, but no one seemed to pay much attention. Hell, everybody at the table had been going at it hot and heavy the night before, thought Longarm. He and Emmaline didn't have any reason to be ashamed or embarrassed.

"This morning I'll give you a better tour of the place," Sir Alfred promised, and Longarm nodded.

"I'd like that," he said. What he really meant was that he wanted to get Sir Alfred alone so that they could hash out the details of the job that had brought Longarm here.

A few minutes later, Ulrich Ganz stumbled into the dining room. He looked tired. Clearly, he hadn't slept well on the cot set up in the storage room. He glared at Brundage and said, "Am I to assume that you will feed me before you send me on my way?"

"That's the civilized thing to do," Brundage said mildly. "Please, sit down, Dr. Ganz. Enjoy your meal, and then I'll have Oscar drive you into Trinidad so that you can catch the next train."

Ganz grumbled, but he took one of the empty seats. He drank some of the green liquid without making faces, and even seemed to enjoy it, Longarm saw. Obviously, Ganz hadn't been raised on good old American food.

Longarm finished his meal, surprising himself by scraping up the last of the gruel with his spoon. He pushed away what was left of the vegetable drink, however. Most of the other guests had already left the table, since they had started eating before Longarm did. Emmaline was left, along with Ganz and Lady Margaret and Mark Hanley.

Lady Margaret caught hold of Hanley's hand and stood up. "Come along, Mark," she ordered. "I want another massage."

"I gave you a massage before breakfast," Hanley protested.

"And now I want another one." Lady Margaret tugged on him, and Hanley went grudgingly.

Sir Alfred patted his lips with a napkin, then said, "Mr. Parker, if you'd care to come with me to my library, I'd love to show you some of my treatises on bodily cleansing to begin your tour."

Longarm knew what Brundage meant by that, and he was just as anxious to talk to the little scientist in private as Brundage was to have the conversation. However, that would leave Emmaline alone here in the dining room with Ganz. Longarm glanced toward her and frowned slightly, unsure how to proceed.

Oscar saved him from having to make that decision by walking in at that moment. The driver and handyman sat down in a chair by the wall, cocked his right ankle on his left knee, and thumbed back his Stetson. "I'll wait right here for you, Dr. Ganz," he told the Prussian. Ganz just grunted.

Longarm wasn't nearly as worried about Emmaline with Oscar around. Oscar had a .45 on his hip and was leathery enough that Longarm was confident he knew how to use it. Ganz wouldn't try to bother Emmaline as long as Oscar was in the room.

"Be glad to take a look at them books of yours, Sir Alfred," Longarm said as he stood up. He added in an undertone to Emmaline, "See you later," and she nodded in agreement.

Brundage led Longarm down a corridor and into a room that was lined from floor to ceiling with bookshelves. It would have been a dark, gloomy place if not for the large window on the east wall. The curtains were open, letting the morning sun shine in.

Sir Alfred made sure the thick door was closed, then turned to Longarm and said, "You're the gentleman from the federal government, I take it?"

"U.S. Deputy Marshal Custis Long," Longarm told him.

"Are you carrying identification?"

Longarm shook his head. "My boss, Billy Vail, told me not to, since I'm working in secret, so I left my badge and bona fides back in Denver. But he said to tell you 'Nottingham,' whatever that means."

Sir Alfred smiled. "That was the code word I requested the government operative use to identify himself when he arrived. I was fairly certain last night that you were the lawman. Now I'm sure."

Longarm reached for a cheroot. "Now that we've got that out of the way, tell me what's going on here, Sir Alfred. The way I understand it, somebody's been trying to ambush you."

Quickly, Brundage held up a hand. "Please, Mr. Parker— I shall continue to call you by that name, if you'll allow that, so as not to slip and expose your true identity—but smoking tobacco is not allowed here at Briarcliff Manor."

Longarm frowned. "You don't eat meat, drink coffee, or smoke?"

"We don't indulge in the imbibing of alcoholic beverages either," Brundage said with a slight smile.

"Good Lord!" exclaimed Longarm. "What *do* you do?"

"We try to concentrate on the pleasures of the flesh that have an actual beneficial effect."

"Oh, yeah," said Longarm, remembering what he and Emmaline had done the night before, as well as all the things he had heard going on behind the other closed doors. He pushed that out of his mind and went on. "So, tell me about what happened to make you holler for help from Uncle Sam."

"Very well." Sir Alfred's expression grew solemn. "Simply put, I believe someone is trying to kill me."

"I got that idea from my boss. How about some details?"

"Certainly." Brundage sank into a chair behind the desk and gestured at a comfortable-looking armchair in front of it. "Sit down, please, Mr. Parker." When Longarm had done so, the Englishman went on. "It began about a month ago. I was on a hike through the foothills near here when I was nearly caught in a rock slide. I'm sure I would have been badly injured, if not killed, had I not been able to avoid the falling rocks by ducking into a crevice in the hillside."

"You go on hikes very often?"

"Two or three times each week. I like to commune with nature."

Longarm nodded. "You go on these strolls at the same time?"

"Oh, no," Brundage replied with a shake of his head. "Just when the spirit moves me and I feel a need for such a constitutional."

"But anybody could have seen you leaving and figured out what you were doing, even followed you?"

"Certainly. I don't skulk out when I leave."

Longarm rasped a thumbnail along the line of his jaw as he thought about that. It didn't have to mean anything. Rock slides happened in the foothills all the time. But someone *could* have started the one that had nearly crushed Sir Alfred, he supposed.

"What else?" he said.

"I went for a ride one day about a week after that, and the horse ran away with me. I'm sure I could have been badly injured if I had taken a fall."

"You ride much?"

"Not these days. But I *am* an expert rider, Mr. Parker, if that's what you're getting at. I often rode to the hounds when I was a young man in England. What caused the trouble here was that someone placed a piece of metal under the saddle where it would gall the horse and make it bolt. It rubbed a bad sore on the poor animal."

Well, that sounded less like an accident than the rock slide, all right, thought Longarm. "Anything else?"

"My word, yes. There was the gunshot."

"Gunshot?" echoed Longarm.

Brundage turned in his chair and pointed at the window behind him. "The bullet came in there and broke a pane of glass. Then it went through the back of my chair here"— he put his finger in a small hole in the upholstery that Longarm hadn't noticed before—"and went on across the room to imbed itself in the books. It ruined a perfectly good first edition of Hawthorne, in fact."

Longarm stood up and peered through the window. Sir Alfred had obviously had the broken pane replaced. He could see the valley spreading out before him, and on the far side of it, the road that climbed back up on its way through the foothills and on to Trinidad.

"Lots of places out there where a fella could've taken a potshot at you," he said.

"Indeed."

"What time of day was it?"

"Just after dusk. My lamps were burning in here, but I hadn't yet drawn the curtains."

Longarm nodded slowly. "The bushwhacker saw you sit down at the desk and drew a bead on the back of your chair. How much did the slug miss you by?"

Brundage swallowed, and Longarm thought he was a bit paler now than he had been a moment earlier. "No more than three inches, I'd say. I attempted to figure the angles and vectors, but I'm not really a geometrician."

"Where was the book it hit?"

Sir Alfred came around the desk and went over to the shelves, crouching to point to one of the leather-bound volumes. "Right here. I replaced the damaged book with a copy of Bulwer-Lytton."

Longarm went over to the shelves, hunkered down, and squinted back along the path of the bullet. After a moment, he nodded. "The fella was up yonder on the road. A long shot, but not impossible. You still got the slug?"

Brundage went to the desk and opened a drawer. He took out a misshapen lump of lead that he dropped in Longarm's palm. Longarm tried to judge the weight of it.

"Could've come from an old buffalo gun," he said. "I don't think it's from a Winchester. Too heavy for that, probably .50-caliber."

"I bow to your superior knowledge on such matters, Mr. Parker," said Brundage.

"I'll just hang on to this," Longarm said as he tucked the slug into his vest pocket. "Anything else?"

Brundage shook his head. "No, but aren't those three incidents sufficient proof that someone is trying to do me harm?"

"Don't know about the rock slide, but the business with the horse and the shot through the window weren't accidents," Longarm agreed. "Got any ideas about who'd want you dead, Sir Alfred?"

"Only one." Brundage took a deep breath. "I hate to accuse a man without proof, but I think Obadiah Jones is responsible for the attempts on my life."

"The reverend from Trinidad?"

"That's right. Oscar told me that Reverend Jones accosted you and the other passengers on the wagon yesterday evening after the train arrived."

"He did some sin-shouting, sure enough," said Longarm. "Called this place a den of iniquity, if I recollect right. Said something about you being a minion of Satan."

Sir Alfred sighed. "Yes, that sounds like the good reverend. He simply refuses to believe that the pleasures of the body can be spiritual as well as physical. Why, the Good Lord wouldn't have given us these bodies and the desires that go with them had He not intended for us to make use of them!"

Longarm hadn't come here to debate such things. He asked, "How does Jones know anything about what goes on out here in the first place? He don't strike me as the sort who'd come for a health cure."

"No, not at all," Brundage agreed. "His daughter Alice worked here as a maid for a short time. It's impossible to keep the various activities a secret from the servants, even if we want to. I suppose Alice went back to her father and told him about the things she had seen and heard while she was employed here."

Longarm nodded. It was all fitting together. He said, "If I can borrow one of your saddle horses, I'll take a ride into Trinidad and do some nosing around."

"Certainly." Sir Alfred hesitated, then asked, "How shall I explain your absence to Emmaline? I sense that the two of you have grown rather . . . close?"

Emmaline was a problem, all right, Longarm thought with a frown. If he disappeared all day, she would wonder where he was. Not to mention that business of Ganz trying to steal her skull. . . .

But Ganz was leaving this morning, Longarm recalled, and that eased his mind somewhat. No one else at Briarcliff Manor knew about the Baumhofer Cranium except for Sir Alfred, and Longarm didn't think he was any threat.

"I know," Sir Alfred said. "I shall tell her that you're in

one of the meditation rooms and cannot be disturbed until evening. How would that be?"

"Meditation rooms?" repeated Longarm.

"Yes, we have several small chambers where the walls are so thick that no sound can pass in or out. Nor are there any windows to distract the occupant, and the only furnishing is a small pallet on the floor. One lays there in the silence and darkness and totally clears one's mind."

It didn't sound like much fun to Longarm. In fact, it sounded sort of like solitary confinement at Yuma Prison. But he nodded and said, "All right, you can tell her I'm in one of those whatever you called 'em, meditation rooms. I ought to be back from Trinidad before dark. Is there a back way in and out of the stables, so nobody will see me coming and going?"

Sir Alfred nodded. "Yes, there's a trail that leads out the far end of the valley. One branch of it then circles back around to the main road. Bear to the right when you come to the fork. What is it exactly that you hope to discover?"

"I'm not rightly sure," Longarm admitted. "But I reckon I'll know it when I see it."

Chapter 7

Sir Alfred gave Longarm directions for getting to the stable, and then Longarm went back up to his room for a few minutes before leaving Briarcliff Manor. He hoped he wouldn't run into Emmaline on the way, because he didn't want to explain what he was doing. Luck was with him: The second-floor corridor was deserted as he slipped back into his room. He took his rolled-up shell belt and the holstered Colt from his carpetbag and carried them in his Stetson as he left the room. Again, no one was in the hallway.

He went down the outside staircase to the garden. Laughter filled the air, along with splashing from the mineral baths. Longarm ducked behind a hedge so that none of the patients cavorting in the baths would see him as he made his way to the stable, which was beyond the garden. When he was out of sight of the house, he took the gunbelt from inside his hat and strapped it on, then settled the Stetson on his head. Feeling fully dressed for the first time since arriving at Briarcliff Manor, he strode on to the stable.

The hostler working there introduced himself as Jed. He was skinny and middle-aged, probably another former cowboy like Oscar who had found himself working here for one reason or another. He must've sensed a fellow Westerner in Longarm, however, because he allowed himself a grin as he said, "Don't hardly seem like you fit in with that bunch up yonder at the main house, Mr. Parker."

"Can you keep a secret, Jed?" asked Longarm.

The hostler leaned forward eagerly. "I reckon I can."

Longarm said in a confidential tone, "I'm just as crazy as they are, only in different ways."

Jed slapped his thigh and cackled with laughter. "Ain't we all!" he exclaimed. "You say you're needin' a saddle hoss, Mr. Parker?"

"That's right," said Longarm. He leaned on the corral fence and nodded toward one of the animals inside. "What about that big, ugly, lineback dun?"

Jed laughed again. "Best hoss in the lot, though he ain't much for looks. You got a good eye for horseflesh."

"Dab a loop on him for me. Saddles in the tack room?"

"Yep. He'p yourself."

Within a few minutes, Longarm had the dun saddled and ready to go. He swung up onto the horse's back and settled down into the stockman's saddle, the only kind that he had found in the tack room. He normally rode a McClellan, but he'd spent enough time cowboying after coming west so that he had no trouble with a regular saddle. He nodded a farewell to Jed, then set out on the trail that led to the far end of the valley.

The scenery in these parts was pretty, no doubt about it, with the lush green valleys of the foothills overlooked by the rocky, snowcapped peaks of the mountains. Longarm's mind was on other things besides the view, however. He was thinking about the job that had brought him here.

The part of the assignment concerning Mark Hanley had been no trouble so far. And if Lady Margaret had her way, doubtless she would keep Hanley so worn out from lovemaking that he wouldn't be able to get into any scrapes. The attempted murder of Sir Alfred Brundage was a different story. That bothered Longarm. Even if Obadiah Jones was behind the rock slide, the bushwhacking, and the runaway horse, Longarm would still have to find proof.

Once he had some evidence, then he could arrest Jones. The fact that Jones was a preacher bothered Longarm a little, but if Jones had indeed taken that shot at Brundage and done the other things, then he had crossed the line. He would no longer be a minister in Longarm's eyes, but a would-be killer just like any other backshooting bushwhacker.

Longarm came to the spot where the trail forked. He took the right-hand turn, just as Sir Alfred had told him, and after an hour of looping around through the foothills, the trail joined the main road again. Less than an hour after that, Longarm rode down into Trinidad.

If he'd had his badge and identification papers with him, the easiest thing to do would have been to contact the local sheriff, lay out the situation, and ask the man about Obadiah Jones. From what Longarm had seen, the sheriff was quite familiar with Jones's tendency toward troublemaking where anybody connected with Briarcliff Manor was concerned. Longarm could still talk to the local star packer and try to convince the man that he was a fellow lawman, but he would hold that in reserve in case he couldn't find out anything about Jones in any other way.

When in doubt, Longarm told himself as he reined in at a hitch rack, head for the nearest saloon. And that was exactly where he found himself, in front of an establishment known as the Gold Dust. The doors were open, and player-piano music tinkled merrily from beyond the bat-wings.

Longarm looped the dun's reins around the hitch rack and stepped up onto the boardwalk. As he shouldered through the bat-wings and stepped inside the saloon, a potent combination of odors filled his nostrils. It was composed of tobacco smoke, sawdust, stale beer, whiskey, and human flesh. Not the prettiest smell in the world, but one with which Longarm was extremely familiar, since he had experienced it in hundreds of saloons, gambling dens, and whorehouses across the West.

The main room of the Gold Dust was long and narrow,

with a mahogany bar running along the right-hand wall. At mid-morning like this, the place wasn't crowded, but there were half a dozen drinkers on hand, four of them sitting at a table, the other two leaning on the bar. Behind the bar, a bald-headed drink juggler wearing a bow tie and a grayish shirt that had once been white ran a rag over the hardwood in lazy circles. Despite the music from the player piano in the back of the room, there wasn't a woman in sight to dance with. Men who came to a saloon at this hour of day were more interested in doing some serious drinking than they were in female companionship.

The bartender looked up and nodded to Longarm without any real interest. "Mornin'," he said. "Something I can get for you?"

"Beer," said Longarm. He propped a foot on the brass rail along the bottom of the bar. The bartender filled a glass with beer from a tap and cut off the head with a little wooden paddle, then set it in front of Longarm.

"That'll be a nickel."

Longarm dropped a half-dollar on the bar. "I'll probably use most of this." He sipped the beer, and found it surprisingly cold.

"Don't recollect seeing you around before," said the bartender. The tone of his voice made it clear he was making conversation out of habit, not because he was really interested in anything Longarm had to say.

"Came into town yesterday on the train." Longarm decided to tell part of the truth. "I'm staying out at Briarcliff Manor."

That made the bartender's eyes widen, and his nonchalant attitude fell away from him. "That crazy Englishman's place?"

"Well, it's run by Sir Alfred Brundage. I couldn't say how crazy he is or isn't. Don't know the fella that well yet."

One of the other men at the bar leaned toward Longarm. "Say, is it true what I've heard about that place?" he asked.

Longarm took another sip of beer. "Depends on what you've heard."

A lecherous grin spread across the townie's florid face. "That it's nothin' more'n a fancy, high-priced whorehouse."

"Yeah," put in the bartender, "folks say that just about everything under the sun goes on out there, that a fella can bed down with any of the other guests he wants to." The bartender licked his lips. "Two or three at a time even, if that's what he wants."

"Well, I've only been there one night," Longarm said dryly, "but you couldn't prove that by me."

And that was true enough, he thought. Emmaline had been plenty to satisfy him the night before. If he'd had a couple more women there, he wasn't sure what he would have done with them.

Might have been downright entertaining to try to figure it out, though, he mused.

A couple of the men at the table got up and came over to the bar, having heard what the conversation was about. One of them said, "Tell us about the other guests, mister. Are all the women beautiful?"

"I wouldn't say that," Longarm replied truthfully. "Most of 'em just look like normal women."

"That's good enough for me," one of the men said with a laugh.

Longarm put a frown on his face. "How is it you boys know so much about what goes on out there at Briarcliff Manor?"

"We've heard stories."

"Lots of stories," added one of the other men.

"Reverend Jones, down at the Holiness church, is all the time rantin' and ravin' about that place," said the bartender. "His daughter worked out there for a while, you know."

One of the men laughed. "Old Obadiah was probably afraid Alice was gettin' it put to *her* too."

Longarm said, "This Reverend Jones, would he be a tall,

71

skinny fella, wears a black suit and hat all the time and waves a bible?"

"That would describe a lot of preachers, mister, but yeah, that's Obadiah, all right," said the bartender.

"Thought as much," Longarm said with a nod. "We ran into him yesterday evening when me and some of the other guests were leaving town in the wagon Sir Alfred sent for us."

"Yeah, I heard about that," said one of the men. "Oscar Lawton threatened to whip the reverend, or something like that."

"Oscar probably could," another man said.

"I don't know," said Longarm. "Preacher or not, Jones looked like a pretty salty hombre to me."

"Well, I reckon he is. Or was anyway. Used to be a buffalo hunter down in the Panhandle, 'bout ten years ago."

Longarm didn't let them see how interested he was in that bit of information. "Is that so?" he asked casually.

"Yep. I've heard tell he downed thousands of those shaggy critters."

"Must be a good shot then," Longarm commented.

All the men nodded. One of them said, "I think he's still got that old Sharps Big Fifty of his. Course, he doesn't use it anymore, since he took up preachin' and all."

Longarm wasn't so sure about that. In fact, it was looking more and more as if Obadiah Jones had indeed used his old Sharps buffalo rifle recently—to put a hole in Sir Alfred's window, chair, and first edition of Hawthorne. And damned near in Sir Alfred's head. . . .

Longarm drained the rest of his beer. Maybe it was time to pay a visit to the good reverend.

He waved off the bartender's offer of change from the fifty-cent piece, and ignored the pleas from the townies to tell them more of the lurid details of the goings-on at Briarcliff Manor. Longarm left the Gold Dust and spoke to the first woman he encountered on the boardwalk, tugging on the brim of his Stetson as he asked her where he could find the Reverend Jones's church. The woman pointed up the slight incline of Trinidad's main street to a whitewashed building that stood on the edge of town. There was no steeple on the building, but other than that it looked like a church, all right.

Longarm thanked the woman and then strolled along the street until he reached the church. The front door was unlocked. He opened it and stepped into the hushed interior of the sanctuary.

There were pews on both sides of the room with an aisle down the center. At the front of the room was a raised podium made out of pine boards. To the left of the podium was a door leading to the rear of the church; to the right was an old piano. The place was empty.

Longarm called, "Anybody home?" making sure his voice was loud enough to be heard in the back room. A moment later the door near the podium opened and a young woman stepped out.

Immediately, Longarm recognized her as Alice Jones. He had seen her the evening before when she had fetched the sheriff to corral her father, and he had heard the local badge call her by name. She was about twenty years old, Longarm judged, with long, light brown hair. She was wearing a shapeless gray dress, but its shapelessness didn't completely conceal the curves of the body underneath it. Alice was pretty, maybe even beautiful, in a fresh, well-scrubbed way. Longarm could understand why her father would worry about her working in a manor house full of rich folks who were being encouraged to indulge their every sexual whim.

"Hello," she said now, clearly somewhat surprised to see Longarm. He wondered if she recognized him from the previous evening, as he did her. A second later he got the answer to that question as she went on. "You're one of the people Oscar took out to Briarcliff last night, aren't you?"

"That's right," Longarm said. He reached up and took his hat off, seeing as how he was not only in the House of

73

the Lord but was also talking to a lady. "And you're Miss Jones."

"If you're looking for my father, he's not here right now. He's out visiting the sick." A worried tone came into her voice as she continued. "Besides, we don't need any trouble."

"Wasn't intending to make any," Longarm told her. "I just want to talk to him, maybe find out why he's so upset about Sir Alfred and Briarcliff Manor."

"You know why," Alice said without hesitation. "If you've spent even one night in that house, you know what goes on out there. It . . . it's scandalous, the way those people carry on!"

Longarm eased a few steps closer to her. "I understand you used to work out there, ma'am."

"Only for a short time, until I found out what it was really like." She was breathing faster now, her breasts rising and falling under the gray dress. "All those people and their . . . their carnal urges. Doing whatever they feel like doing, sometimes right out in the open where anybody could watch them . . . I never saw such things . . . and the way they . . . they expect everyone to take part in their sinful couplings . . . groping and putting their hands all over a person's body . . . and not just the men, that would have been bad enough, but the women too . . ."

Alice's face was flushed nearly as red as the sunset by now as she described the activities at Briarcliff Manor, and to tell the truth, Longarm was getting a mite overheated himself. He held up a hand to stop her and said, "Yes, ma'am, I know. I reckon you told your pa all about it, and that's what got him so riled up about Sir Alfred?"

"What business is that of yours?" Alice asked sharply. "You're one of Mr. Brundage's guests. You must know all about the situation."

"I know your pa has caused enough trouble in the past to get the sheriff involved," Longarm said. "As a matter of fact, you were the one who fetched the law yesterday evening, weren't you?"

"Mr. Brundage threatened to have my father thrown in jail if he kept bothering the guests when they came in on the train. I just didn't want to see that happen. No one wants to see their father behind bars."

Longarm couldn't argue with that. He said, "So you're just as upset by what goes on at Briarcliff Manor as the reverend is?" A woman could pull the trigger on a rifle as well as a man could, he was thinking, although it would take a mighty strong woman to handle one of those Big Fifties. Still, Alice Jones had been raised around buffalo guns, so it wasn't unreasonable to think that she might be able to use one.

She shook her head, though, and said, "No, I wouldn't go that far. I suppose Mr. Brundage and his guests have the right to do anything they want to out there, as long as they don't force anybody to join in with them who doesn't want to."

"Does that ever happen?" asked Longarm.

"Well . . . no. At least not while I was there. Any time one of the guests tried to bother me, Mr. Brundage let them know right away that the servants were just there to work."

That answer weakened the potential case Longarm was building in his mind against Alice, but it didn't make him disregard her completely as a suspect. However, it was still much more likely her father had been responsible for Sir Alfred's troubles.

"I still don't understand why you're here asking all these questions," Alice went on when Longarm didn't say anything. "Aren't you one of them?"

"Them?"

"Those . . . those rich people who come out there as guests. The ones who think they can do anything they want and get away with it."

Longarm shook his head. "I'm staying at Briarcliff Manor, all right, but I'm just trying to figure things out."

Alice moved closer to him. "Are the guests still . . . still doing the things they've always done?"

"I don't reckon I know what you mean," said Longarm, even though he knew very well what she was getting at. He ought to be ashamed of himself for stringing her along, he thought.

"You know . . . getting in bed with each other and indulging the lusts of the flesh."

She started to breathe faster again, Longarm noted.

"I saw them sometimes, you know," Alice went on. "It was awful, just dreadful. Those men's things were so big, and they put them in the women every which way. . . ."

Maybe it was high time for him to leave, thought Longarm. He hadn't gotten to talk to Reverend Jones, but he supposed that could wait. He didn't want to just stand here while Alice talked herself into a frenzy, especially not when he himself was beginning to show a physical reaction to her heated, breathy voice. . . .

Longarm didn't have to worry about that, because at that moment the doors of the church banged open behind him, and Obadiah Jones's angry voice yelled, "What in the name of all that's holy is going on here?"

Chapter 8

Longarm started to swing around, and as he did so, Jones went on. "Step away from my daughter, you heathen!"

That wasn't hardly fair, thought Longarm. Jones hadn't even gotten a good enough look at him yet to recognize him, and already the preacher considered him a heathen.

Not that that opinion was likely to change once Jones realized Longarm was one of the people who had been in the wagon bound for Briarcliff Manor the day before.

Jones started to stalk up the aisle between the pews as Longarm said, "Howdy, Reverend. I didn't mean any harm by coming here—"

"You!" Jones interrupted loudly. "I know you! You're one of those sinners who inhabit that palace of lust! A denizen of the valley of sin!"

Clearly, Jones was one of those gents who never talked in a normal tone of voice when he could yell instead. Longarm held up both hands, palms out, as he said, "I was just about to leave, Reverend—"

"The Lord shall smite the wicked!" bellowed Jones. "And I am the instrument of the Lord!"

He had his bible clutched in his left hand. His right clenched into a bony fist, which he swung at Longarm's head as he lunged forward toward the podium.

"Pa! No!" shouted Alice, but her father ignored her, continuing his charge.

Jones's punch was long, looping, and so slow that Longarm had no trouble ducking under it. He stepped inside and grabbed the minister around the waist. "Dang it, Reverend, hold on there!" he said. "I didn't come here to fight."

Jones stomped hard on Longarm's right foot, causing Longarm to let go of him and hop back a step while grimacing in pain. The preacher swung his fist again, this time in a backhand that cracked across Longarm's cheek, staggering him. Jones might be skinny, but he had plenty of strength in his wiry body.

Longarm had as much respect for ministers as the next fella, but he wasn't going to stand around and let anybody whale on him just because the hombre was carrying the Good Book. As Jones lunged toward him again, Longarm blocked the preacher's swing with his left forearm and shot a hard, swift right into Jones's face. The blow landed solidly, rocking Jones's head back and straightening his body. Longarm hooked a left into the man's midsection, doubling him over, but then a wildcat landed on his back before he could do anything else.

Alice yelled, "Leave my pa alone!" as she flailed at Longarm's head. Her legs locked around his waist, and she tangled the fingers of one hand in his hair as she struck at him with the other.

Longarm spun around and gave a little hop, thinking that he must look like a bucking bronc trying to dislodge the rider on its back. Alice stuck to him like a burr, though, so he was forced to reach back and catch hold of her. He grabbed her dress, and as he heaved, he heard a ripping sound.

Her grip on him came loose, and she slid off his back to go tumbling into the aisle. Longarm saw that her dress was torn at one shoulder, the fabric falling down so that her shoulder and upper arm were exposed.

The rush of footsteps warned him that Alice's father was coming back for more. Longarm whirled around in time to see that Reverend Jones was practically on top of him, a gaunt, furious scarecrow of a man. Jones had dropped his bible, so he was able to windmill both fists at Longarm.

Longarm dived under the wild punches and slammed his shoulder into Jones's belly. The preacher went over backward, with Longarm landing heavily on top of him. That knocked the wind out of Jones and left him lying there, writhing and gasping for air, as Longarm scrambled back to his feet. He turned quickly toward Alice in case she was about to jump him again.

All the fight had gone out of her, though. She had managed to catch hold of one of the pews and pull herself upright, but she was just standing there leaning on the pew and shaking her head slowly. Longarm looked around for his hat, spotted it on the floor, and bent to retrieve it. While he knocked it back into shape and settled it on his head, he said, "I really didn't come here to cause trouble, ma'am."

"H-harlot!" Jones screeched from the floor. "Cover yourself, girl! The shame of it, to stand with wanton flesh exposed in the House of the Lord!"

There wasn't anything particularly wanton about a bare shoulder, thought Longarm, although in Alice Jones's case, the flesh revealed by the torn dress *was* rather smooth and creamy. He put that thought out of his head and turned back to Jones, who was struggling to stand up. The preacher's hat had been knocked off in the fracas, and his thin gray hair was askew. He looked mostly pathetic now, rather than somber and menacing.

But that didn't mean he wasn't a would-be killer, Longarm reminded himself.

Still, he didn't want to accuse Jones outright of being the bushwhacker. That would mean revealing his identity as a lawman, and if Jones *wasn't* the culprit, Longarm would have lost his ability to work in secret. So he said,

"All I wanted to do was talk to you about buffalo hunting, Reverend."

Jones blinked in surprise as he finally managed to straighten up. "Buffalo hunting?" he repeated as he stared at Longarm.

"That's right. I heard that you used to be a hunter down in the Panhandle. Thought you might have known some friends of mine."

"Who do you mean?" asked Jones. His voice had dropped to a more normal tone. Evidently, confusion kept him from shouting as much.

"Billy Dixon, Bat Masterson, Bob Pryor and Celestino Mireles, a big fella named Gilworth," said Longarm, naming some buffalo hunters he knew personally and some he knew of only by reputation.

Jones rubbed his jaw, the bony fingers rasping over the gray stubble that grew there. "I knew those men and others," he admitted, "before I found the Lord and gave up the job of killin' His creatures. They were good men, despite the ugliness of their profession."

Longarm nodded. "You see, Reverend, that's all I wanted, just to talk about the old days. I did a little hunting myself a few years back."

"Out of Dodge City?"

"That's right. Worked for the Moore brothers." That was an outright lie, of course, but Longarm had talked to enough veterans of the buffalo hunting days in the Texas Panhandle that he thought he could bluff his way through.

Jones's expression suddenly darkened. "Those were wicked, sinful days. Men soddened themselves with hard liquor and consorted with fallen women. Debauchery, pure debauchery, that's what it was." His voice rose. "Like the evil that transpires out at that abomination of Satan where you're staying, sir!"

"Pa, don't start again," Alice said wearily.

Jones's head snapped around toward her. "I told you to cover yourself!"

"All right, I'm going," she said. She looked at Longarm and added quietly, "I'd take it kindly if you wouldn't come back here and stir him up again, mister." She went through the door into the back room and closed it behind her.

Longarm turned his attention back to Jones, hoping to distract the man from his preaching again before he could get properly wound up. "Do you still have your old buffalo rifle?" he asked.

"I have put away the things of man and taken up the things of God," replied Jones. He picked up the bible from where he had dropped it and brandished the black, leather-bound volume at Longarm.

"Somebody told me you still have your old Big Fifty," Longarm persisted.

"What if I do?"

"I might like to buy it from you," said Longarm, the idea occurring to him abruptly. "Wouldn't mind having a souvenir from those days."

Jones shook his head. "The gun's not for sale."

"Then you do have it."

"I do. But I'll not sell it."

"Could I at least take a look at it?" Longarm knew he was pushing hard, and if Jones was indeed the bush-whacker, he might be getting suspicious by now about this stranger's interest in the heavy Sharps rifle.

"If I show it to you, will you leave?"

"Sure," said Longarm.

Jones sighed. "Come with me then."

He led Longarm into the rear of the church, through the door into a short hall with a door on either side. The one on the left must have been Alice's room, because Jones took Longarm into the chamber on the right, a small, spartanly furnished room. There was only an uncomfortable-looking bed, a straight chair, and a long wooden trunk. Jones lifted the lid of the trunk.

Inside was a bulky, furry item that Longarm recognized as a coat made from a buffalo hide. Beneath it was a long, oilcloth-wrapped bundle. Jones took it out, closed the lid, and placed the bundle on top of the trunk. He unwrapped it gently, his care of the gun revealing perhaps more than he realized. As the Big Fifty was uncovered, Longarm saw that it was in excellent shape.

A man could use it to put a bullet in an enemy's back with no trouble at all.

Jones lifted the rifle, cradling it in his hands, and held it out to Longarm. The big lawman took the weapon and studied it admiringly. "Beautiful," he murmured. He smelled the sharp tang of gun oil. Someone had cleaned the Sharps, and recently too.

There went one of his hopes. He had thought that if the bushwhacker had not cleaned the gun after taking that potshot at Brundage, he would be able to tell that it had been fired in the past few weeks. That would have been one more bit of circumstantial evidence. However, with the Sharps having been freshly cleaned, there was no way of telling when it had been fired last.

Longarm handed the gun back to Jones. "Thank you," he said. "That brings back a lot of memories."

"Sinful ones, I'd guess," said Jones with a disparaging sniff.

Longarm shrugged. "I reckon some people could look at it that way."

"Sin is sin. It is not open to interpretation."

"You're probably right about that, Reverend. Me, I've always cottoned to what the old hymn says: Further along we'll know more about it."

Jones wrapped the rifle in its oilcloth shroud once again and replaced it in the trunk under the buffalo hide coat. "I'll thank you to leave now," he said, "but you're always welcome to come back and pray and worship with us. All sinners are welcome."

"Much obliged for the invite. I'll think about it."

"You do that," said Jones. "Think long and hard about

it, my friend, because what's at stake here is your own immortal soul."

Longarm had left the church before he realized that had sounded vaguely like a threat.

As he walked back down the street, he thought about what he had discovered today and tried not to be depressed about how little it added up to. He had confirmed, at least in his own mind, that Obadiah Jones was probably crazy enough—or fervent enough, if somebody wanted to look at it that way—to have taken a shot at Sir Alfred. The preacher could have followed that back trail into the valley where Briarcliff Manor was located and lurked around until he saw the chance to start that rock slide too, and Longarm couldn't eliminate the possibility that Jones had sneaked into the stable and slipped that galling piece of metal into the saddle as well. That was trickier, though. There would have been more chance of discovery, and it would have been difficult for Jones to know exactly which saddle would be put on Sir Alfred's horse. Not impossible, though, Longarm concluded.

Nor was it impossible that Alice could have done all those things. Longarm considered it more unlikely, but he wasn't ready to rule her out as a suspect. Clearly, she had been aroused by the things she had seen at Briarcliff Manor, and if she felt guilty enough about what seemed to Longarm a natural reaction, she might have tried to eliminate temptation by eliminating the man she blamed for it—Sir Alfred Brundage.

Those were mighty deep waters, Longarm thought with a frown. He preferred cases where criminals were motivated by good old-fashioned greed or some such.

He found himself in front of the sheriff's office, and on a whim, he went inside. The lawman was at his desk scribbling on a piece of paper. He glanced up as Longarm entered, then put the pen aside and stood up. "Can I help you?" he asked.

"Custis Parker," Longarm said as he advanced toward the desk and held out his hand. As he shook hands with the sheriff, he looked around at the office. It was like hundreds of other local law offices he'd been in; a couple of desks, a gun rack on the wall with several shotguns and Winchesters in it, a potbellied stove with a coffeepot sitting on it, a couple of chairs, and an old sofa along one wall. "I'm staying out at Briarcliff Manor."

The sheriff grunted. "Thought I recognized you from that little incident with Obadiah Jones yesterday evening. He bother you again, did he?"

"Nope," Longarm replied with a shake of his head.

"Well, then, what can I do for you?" the sheriff asked. He gestured at the chair in front of the desk. "Have a seat. I'm Sheriff Banning, by the way. Arch Banning."

The lawman was middle-aged and looked competent. As Longarm sat down, he briefly considered how to play this. He decided not to show all his cards right away. "I'm worried about Sir Alfred Brundage," he said. "He's a friend of mine, and there's something odd going on out yonder at his place."

Banning smiled faintly. "Odd?" he repeated. "At Briarcliff Manor? No offense, Mr. Parker, but I reckon most things that go on out there would be considered odd to your ordinary person. It's sort of like . . . well, a high-class brothel, isn't it?"

Longarm shrugged. "I didn't come here to talk about that, Sheriff. I'm more worried that somebody's trying to do harm to Sir Alfred."

"What do you mean?" Banning asked with a frown. "He hasn't made any official complaint to me."

That was true enough, because Sir Alfred had gone over the local lawman's head straight to the Department of State, which had in turn gone to the Justice Department. And as Billy Vail had told him, Longarm represented Uncle Sam at the moment in this matter. Longarm kept that bit of information to himself, though, as he went on. "I think that preacher's trying to kill Sir Alfred." There was just the right tone of concerned citizen in his voice, he thought.

Banning leaned back in his chair and pressed his palms to the top of the desk. "That's a mighty serious accusation, Mr. Parker. You got anything to back it up?"

"Somebody took a shot at Sir Alfred a while back." Longarm fished the flattened bit of lead from his pocket and leaned forward to place it on the desk in front of Banning. "There's the slug. Looks to me like it came from a buffalo rifle."

Banning picked up the slug and studied it intently for a few seconds. "Could be," he admitted as he set it down on the desk again. "And Obadiah has a Sharps Big Fifty. But I reckon you know that already, don't you, Mr. Parker?"

"I've been doing a little nosing around," Longarm admitted.

"Trying to do my job, you mean." Banning's voice was harsh, almost angry.

"I just don't want to see Sir Alfred get hurt, that's all," Longarm said. "You know Reverend Jones a whole lot better than I do. You saw for yourself how he doesn't like Sir Alfred or anything to do with him. Do you think he's capable of taking a potshot at him?"

Banning's mouth tightened. "I don't like to think bad of any preacher, but . . . hell, Parker, you saw how Obadiah carries on. Brundage *has* complained to me about his guests being harassed, and the law's on his side. I have to put a stop to it when Obadiah starts in like he did yesterday evening. But to bushwhack a man . . . I don't want to believe it."

"But you can't say that Jones wouldn't do it, can you?" Longarm asked cannily.

"Damn it, no, I can't!" Banning pushed back his chair. "I'll have a talk with Obadiah—"

"Do me a favor, Sheriff. Leave me out of it when you talk to him."

"Why should I do that?" asked Banning.

"Because if Jones already considers me a sinner just for being out there at Briarcliff Manor, how do you reckon he'll feel about me if he thinks I accused him of ambushing Sir Alfred? I don't want him backshooting *me*."

Banning hesitated, then shrugged. "All right, I won't mention your name. I'll just say I heard a rumor he might have been involved in taking a shot at Brundage." The sheriff sighed. "It's just going to get him stirred up even worse, you know."

That was sort of what Longarm had in mind, but he didn't tell Banning that. He just stood up and said, "Thanks, Sheriff. I appreciate it. I don't want to see anything bad happen to Sir Alfred."

"Neither do I. I don't necessarily agree with everything he does out there, but I don't want anybody murdered in my county either."

Longarm believed the sheriff was being sincere about that. He nodded and left the office.

He was far from satisfied with the results of his visit to Trinidad, but at least he had smoked the hive a little. Now he could sit back and wait to see what flew out.

The dun was still tied in front of the Gold Dust Saloon. Longarm unhitched the reins and swung up into the saddle. He stopped at a water trough to let the horse get a drink, then rode out of the settlement, heading west toward the Sangre de Cristos.

The previous evening, as dusk was settling down over the land, he hadn't noticed the trail branching off from the main road. Having traveled it earlier today, he had no trouble finding it again. He wondered if Emmaline had missed him. A growl from his stomach reminded him that he should have eaten some lunch before leaving Trinidad. Mired as he was in thoughts about the case, it had completely slipped his mind.

As he followed the narrow trail that circled through the hills toward the far end of the valley where Briarcliff Manor was located, the prodding from Longarm's stomach grew even more insistent. His belly gurgled a little. There was nothing in it except that beer he'd had earlier at the Gold Dust, and before that he'd had only the bowl of mush and the half-cup of vile green liquid at breakfast. Lord, a surrounding of decent grub would taste good right about now, he thought.

His eyes spotted a cluster of berries on a bush at the side of the trail. He would have to take a closer look at them to identify them and make sure they were safe to eat, but maybe they could tide him over until he got back to the manor. He tugged on the reins and turned the horse in the direction of the bush.

That sudden veer saved his life, because an instant later a bullet sizzled through the air only inches from his right ear.

Chapter 9

Longarm launched himself out of the saddle. He was already leaning over slightly, studying the berries, so it was a simple matter to pitch off the horse into the brush. Branches clawed at his face, but he ignored the stinging pain. He heard a deadly rattle of leaves as another slug tore through the bushes near him.

He flattened out on the ground and lay motionless. The brush wouldn't stop a bullet, but it was thick enough along this side of the trail to conceal him. Of course, that wouldn't stop the bushwhacker from raking the entire thicket until one of the shots was bound to find him. Longarm knew he couldn't stay where he was.

Moving slowly and carefully, so as not to disturb the bushes too much, he started crawling away from the trail. Out of habit, he had noted certain features of the terrain through which he was passing before the bullets started flying. There was a stand of pine trees about fifty feet away, and if he could manage to get among them, they would offer him much more substantial protection from the bushwhacker's bullets.

He realized now that he hadn't heard the first shot until after he had thrown himself out of the saddle. Only then had the sound of a distant boom come to his ears. The same had held true since then; first a slug would come tearing through the thicket, then the report of the blast would drift through the air. That meant the ambusher was firing from a good long distance away. And the shots had the dull, heavy sound of a high-caliber rifle too.

Like a Sharps Big Fifty.

Longarm's jaw clenched. He'd wanted to stir things up, but he hadn't figured that Obadiah Jones would come after him this quickly. That was the most likely prospect, however. Jones had had time to get ahead of him and set up this ambush while Longarm was in the sheriff's office talking to Arch Banning. The preacher would have had to guess that Longarm would take the long way around, though, instead of following the main road. That was a little troublesome.

A slug ripped through the brush and thudded into the ground about ten feet to Longarm's right. He grimaced. He could hash out the details later, he told himself. Right now, the important thing was to reach those trees before one of the shots found him. He risked lifting his head to see how far he was from the grove, but it didn't do any good. The brush was too thick for him to see anything. All he could do was keep crawling.

Another bullet slammed into the ground behind him, no more than five feet away. Little clods of dirt kicked up by the impact showered back down on him.

The shots were evenly spaced, several seconds apart. That was another factor indicating a Sharps. The Big Fifty was a single-shot weapon and had to be reloaded every time it was fired. An experienced rifleman could do that in a matter of heartbeats, but it was still slower than firing a repeating rifle. Longarm paused, gathering his muscles, and waited for the next shot.

He listened for the bullet, not the sound of the blast itself. When he heard the distinctive whine of the slug through the air not far away, he suddenly sprang to his feet and lunged forward, breaking into a run. The thick brush held him back a little, but he still managed to get up some speed. The trees were about fifteen feet away, he saw.

Ever since he had surged to his feet, he had been counting to himself. When he hit four, he knew he had pushed his luck as far as it would go. He left his feet in a dive, and as he did so, dirt spurted up into his face as a slug hit the ground right next to him. Even though the bushwhacker had had a clear shot for a second, his aim had been hurried, and he had missed.

Longarm intended to see to it that the bastard didn't get another chance at him.

He hit the ground rolling and came up on his feet again, barely breaking stride. The trees loomed up in front of him and he dashed between two of them. He went down in a crouch, putting the thick trunk of one of the pines between him and the bushwhacker's position. His hand went to the butt of his Colt and slipped the gun from the cross-draw rig. Let the son of a bitch come and root him out of these trees, he thought. Just let him try.

Longarm's pulse was thudding heavily in his temples. Gradually, the pounding slowed to a more normal rate. He edged his head past the trunk of the tree to take a look around.

About three hundred yards ahead of the point where he had heard the first bullet, a knoll crowned with trees rose on the left side of the trail. A slug slammed into a tree trunk ten feet from Longarm, followed an instant later by the sound of the shot. Longarm's eyes narrowed as he peered at the knoll. He thought he saw a tendril of smoke rising from the edge of the trees atop the knoll, but at this distance, his eyes could be playing tricks on him. Still, that was the most likely spot for the bushwhacker to be holed up, he decided. The high ground would give the rifleman a commanding field of fire along a lengthy section of the trail.

The knowledge of where the bushwhacker was probably firing from didn't do Longarm a whole lot of good, however. That knoll was far beyond the reach of his handgun, and he couldn't see any way of sneaking up on the bushwhacker until he was close enough to use the Colt. There was too much open ground around the knoll for that.

The rifleman was still firing, but the thick-trunked pines were an effective shield. The slugs either whipped harmlessly past the trees or wasted their impact on the trunks. Bark flew, and Longarm saw one pine cone literally explode when it was hit by a high-powered bullet, but that was the only damage the ambusher was doing. It was a standoff.

And, as usual in situations like this, the fella with the most patience was going to come out ahead. After about twenty minutes during which the shooting continued steadily, the distant blasts finally stopped. The rifleman could be trying to draw him out, Longarm thought, so he stayed put. Another quarter of an hour dragged by.

Finally, Longarm was rewarded by the faint sound of hoofbeats. Somewhere, a horse was traveling fairly fast. The bushwhacker pulling out? Could be, but it also might still be a trick. Longarm remained where he was, safely hidden in the thick stand of trees.

He waited at least an hour after the final shot had sounded before he ventured out. Even then, he was careful, ready to leap back into the trees at the first sign of danger.

But nothing happened, and with a sigh, he holstered his Colt, picked up his hat from the ground, and started looking for the horse he had been riding earlier. He hoped the dun hadn't taken it into its head to go home. If that was the case, Longarm was going to have a long walk back to Briarcliff Manor. He started trudging, casting a wary eye toward the knoll as he passed it, but no more shots came from the top of it.

He found the dun peacefully cropping grass in a field about half a mile along the trail. His feet already hurt from the walk, even though his boots had lower heels than the kind most cowboys wore, so he was grateful when the horse allowed him to come up and snag the reins. The animal had been spooked by the shooting earlier, Longarm supposed, but by now it had calmed down.

His earlier hunger forgotten, Longarm swung up into the saddle and turned the horse around, riding back toward the knoll. He circled it, and found the slope on the back side to be gentler. Watching the ground for tracks, he rode to the top.

Sure enough, a horse had been tethered up there. He found the spot where a jumble of hoofprints told the story. Not far away, at the edge of the trees, there was a shallow depression in the ground. Just the right size and shape for a man's knee, Longarm judged. The bushwhacker had knelt there and fired. Looking down from these heights, Longarm realized just how much of a shooting gallery the trail had been. He was lucky to have escaped with his life.

There was nothing else to indicate who the bushwhacker might have been. No empty shells; the rifleman had picked up his brass before leaving. No cigarette butts, so evidently the man wasn't a smoker. And there was nothing distinctive about the tracks of the man's horse.

Longarm rode back down the hill and turned toward the valley where Briarcliff Manor was located. He still figured that Obadiah Jones was the most likely choice to have been the bushwhacker, but returning to Trinidad to check the preacher's buffalo gun wouldn't do any good. If Jones was the would-be killer, he would have cleaned the Sharps again by now.

Old Jed, the hostler, came out of the tack room when Longarm got back. "Find what you was lookin' for?" he asked.

Longarm shook his head as he dismounted. "Don't know, and that's the pity of it."

"Hoss behave?"

Longarm patted the dun's shoulder as he began to loosen the cinches. "Yep. Good animal, just like you told me, Jed."

The old man grinned a toothless grin. "If there's one thing *I* know, it's hossflesh," he said.

Longarm didn't feel inclined to argue. He just nodded and started back toward the house, leaving Jed to finish unsaddling and rubbing down the horse. He took off his coat, then the gunbelt, and coiled the belt up and carried it over his left arm. He draped the coat over the weapon so that it couldn't be easily seen, in case he ran into anyone before he reached his room.

That was exactly what happened. As he started up the outside stairs, Emmaline appeared at the top of them. She stopped short and looked down at him in surprise.

"Why, Custis," she said, "Sir Alfred told me you were in one of the meditation rooms and couldn't be disturbed."

"Well, I was until just a little while ago," Longarm lied easily. "But there's only so much of that meditating a fella can take. So I went for a walk through the gardens."

Emmaline smiled. "You were hoping to catch Lady Margaret frolicking in the nude, I imagine."

"The thought never occurred to me," Longarm replied honestly. He'd had other things on his mind today.

"It wouldn't have done you any good if it had," Emmaline told him. "I happen to know that Lady Margaret is upstairs with Mark Hanley."

Longarm held up a hand. "No need to say any more."

"No, you don't understand," Emmaline said with a laugh. "I believe she's trying to teach him how to play whist. Poor Mr. Hanley is about to die of exhaustion, so he begged for a respite."

Longarm chuckled. From what he had seen of Lady Margaret, he could understand why Hanley was getting tuckered out.

"I was just about to go down to the mineral baths and soak for a while," Emmaline went on. "I'd be glad to wait for you if you want to join me."

After the day he'd had, that sounded like a pretty good

idea to Longarm. He said, "I'll just go up and change and be down in a few minutes."

"Oh, there's no need to do that. There are dressing rooms next to the baths." She came down the stairs and linked her left arm with his right. "Come on."

Longarm wished he could have reached his room so that he could put away the six-gun that was hidden under his coat, but Emmaline wasn't going to give him that opportunity. He let her tug him down the stairs and into the gardens. They followed a winding path through the shrubbery and flower beds, and eventually came out on a large open area. A flagstone patio had been put down around several mineral baths, which were evidently natural occurrences fed by thermally heated springs. On the far side of the patio were several small structures made of white-washed stone. A pair of pillars supported porticos over the entrance of each building.

"The dressing rooms are made in the Roman style, you know," Emmaline said.

Longarm didn't, but he was willing to take her word for it. He noticed that all the pools were empty at the moment, and commented, "This place was mighty busy earlier, from the sound of it. I heard a heap of laughing and carrying on."

"Everyone has gone inside to get ready for dinner, I suppose. I don't mind the privacy if you don't, Custis."

"Nope, I don't mind," Longarm said with a grin. He was still hungry, but the cravings weren't as urgent now. The ambush had sort of driven all thoughts of eating out of his head for a while.

And to be honest, when he looked at Emmaline, he felt a craving of an entirely different sort.

She slipped her arm out of his and headed for one of the dressing rooms. "I'll see you in a few minutes," she said.

Longarm nodded, and went to the room next to the one she had picked out. He opened the door and stepped inside, expecting to find a robe or some bathing trunks or something. Instead, there was only a small stone bench and a few hooks on the walls

"There's nothing in here," he called out, knowing Emmaline could hear him next door.

She laughed. "Of course not. You don't wear anything into a mineral bath. You don't want to interfere with your body soaking up all the benefits of the water."

Longarm frowned slightly. If that was the case, it seemed like folks ought to call this an undressing room, rather than a dressing room. He hung his Stetson on one of the hooks, set his coat and the holstered revolver down at one end of the bench, then sat down himself at the other end to remove his boots.

Within a few minutes, he had stripped down to his birthday suit and hung up his clothes. He heard splashing outside, and Emmaline called, "Are you ready, Custis?" Longarm hesitated at the door, not sure if he was ready or not. But he had never been plagued with any sort of false modesty. He took a deep breath, swung the door open, and stepped out, naked as a jaybird.

Emmaline was already in one of the pools. The hot water was bubbling and swirling, and it covered her body for the most part, leaving only the upper swells of her breasts bare. She watched Longarm with an appreciative smile on her face as he strode toward the pool. "You are quite an impressive specimen of the male animal, Custis," she told him.

"Much obliged," he replied, not knowing what else to say under the circumstances. He reached the edge of the pool and stepped down into the murky water, lowering one foot into it rather tentatively. It was hot, all right, but not so hot that he couldn't stand it.

The pool was roughly circular and about fifteen feet in diameter. Steps had been hewn out of the rock, so that Longarm was able to climb easily into it. The steps also served as benches, so he lowered himself onto the one where Emmaline was sitting. He was taller than she was, so more of his chest stuck out of the water.

Emmaline slid over so that her bare hip was pressed against his. "Isn't it wonderful, Custis?" she asked. "So soothing. It's like the water just washes away all your troubles."

Longarm had to admit that it felt pretty good. He leaned back, draping one arm along the edge of the pool and the other around Emmaline's shoulders. He closed his eyes for a moment, allowing himself to relax.

Then he stiffened as she moved her hand under the water and closed her fingers around his manhood.

The shaft instantly began to harden. Longarm started to turn toward Emmaline, but she stopped him by resting her other hand on his chest. "No, don't move," she whispered. "Just sit there and let me do this for you."

"Don't hardly seem fair to let you do all the work," said Longarm.

"Don't worry, you'll have plenty of opportunities to reciprocate."

Longarm planned to reciprocate, all right—and more than once if he got the chance.

He closed his eyes again as she began sliding her palm up and down his rigid pole. The minerals in the pool seemed to make it more slippery than regular water, so Emmaline's fingers glided with maddening smoothness along Longarm's heated flesh. She leaned over so that her mouth could fasten over his right nipple. She tongued it as it grew hard.

Longarm sat there and luxuriated in the sensations she was creating within him. His shaft throbbed and grew to an aching hardness. He felt Emmaline shifting around, but didn't open his eyes to see what she was doing. He figured he would find out soon enough.

She straddled him, her fingers skillfully guiding his erection to the slick opening between her legs. With a teasing slowness that brought a groan from him, she lowered herself onto the shaft, sheathing it inside her an inch at a time. Gradually, Longarm filled her, and a little gasp escaped from her lips as she finally hit bottom. He was as far into her as he could possibly go.

"Emmaline . . . ," he said, passion making his voice raspy.

"Shhh," she whispered. "Just be still, like I told you."

With that, she began to pump her hips back and forth in a languid motion, riding him gently. She put her hands on his cheeks and held his head still as she brought her mouth to his. Her lips were soft and warm, and her tongue thrust slowly in and out of his mouth in a gesture that echoed the way his shaft was sliding back and forth in her femininity.

Longarm had no idea how long they sat there like that, locked together. Emmaline was barely moving, but it was enough to make waves of pleasure crest and break within him. She panted against his mouth, her lips still open and her tongue still probing against his, and he knew she was feeling the same level of arousal, if not more. He wanted to put his arms around her, crush her to him and cup her breasts and suckle those lovely nipples of hers, but she had asked him to let her do this, and Longarm always made a point of it to oblige a lady whenever he had the chance.

His climax hit him so powerfully and unexpectedly that for a second he thought he was going to black out. His hips moved of their own volition, driving his manhood to the ultimate depths again, and he held it there as his seed poured out of him in one wracking surge after another. A huge shudder gripped Emmaline as her own climax rippled through her. Longarm finally folded his arms around her, figuring she wouldn't mind now. She was still trembling as he held her cradled against his broad chest.

"Beautiful," she gasped. "So beautiful . . ."

Something bumped Longarm's foot underneath the waters of the mineral bath.

He caught his breath in surprise, quickly checking to make sure that he hadn't just felt Emmaline's foot. She was still straddling his hips, though, with her legs bent so that her feet were just about even with Longarm's knees.

"Better get out," he said tautly.

"Mmmm. But it feels so *good* here in your arms. . . ."

"Get out of the pool, Emmaline." There was no mistaking the sharp command in his voice. He moved his foot and felt the thing again, heavy and lumpy and soft. He pushed himself up a little in the water, fighting off the atavistic fear that tried to rise up in him as if he were one of Emmaline's Neanderthal men.

She must have realized how serious he was, because she scrambled off him and pulled herself out of the pool, rolling over on the flagstones. "Custis, what is it?" she asked anxiously.

Longarm stood up, torn between the desire to find out what was going on and the impulse to get the hell out of the water. He forced himself to move closer to the thing and reach down, plunging his arm into the water as he felt around beneath the surface. If he was right about what he had felt, there was nothing in the pool that could do him any harm.

His fingers closed on what felt like the collar of a coat. He pulled the heavy weight of the thing—dead weight, he supposed—closer to the edge of the pool. "Get back, Emmaline," he said grimly. As she did so, he got both hands on the thing and heaved it up out of the water, letting it sprawl half in the pool and half on the flagstones.

Emmaline started to scream.

Longarm stood there and stared down bleakly into the ugly, contorted, and definitely dead face of Dr. Ulrich Ganz.

Chapter 10

Longarm found himself wishing that he had a few minutes to think about this grisly discovery before everything got even more confused, but Emmaline's screams didn't give him any chance for that. Oscar came running, pounding through the gardens from the direction of the stable, and as he reached the mineral baths and skidded to a stop on the flagstones, he stared bug-eyed at Ganz's corpse. Oscar's gun was in his hand, and Longarm didn't want his trigger finger getting itchy. "Better put that hogleg away," he advised.

Oscar glanced down at the Colt he was gripping so tightly, then nodded. "Yeah," he said. "Don't look like I'll need it. That fella's already as dead as he's ever going to get, ain't he?"

"That's right," said Longarm. "How'd you know?"

"I've seen a few dead men in my time," replied Oscar. He holstered his revolver. His eyes cut over toward Emmaline for an instant, Longarm noted. She was still stark naked, but Oscar was doing a good job of not staring at her. Not every man would have had so much self-control.

Someone shouted, "I say! What's wrong over there?" Other voices echoed the question. People were coming from the mansion now to see what was wrong, their attention drawn by Emmaline's screams.

She had fallen silent, but like Longarm and Oscar, she was still staring at Ganz's waterlogged body. Horror was etched on her features.

"Better go get dressed before a whole passel of folks swarms all over us," Longarm told her.

For a second, Emmaline didn't react. Then she nodded numbly and started toward the dressing room where she had left her clothes.

"Wouldn't mind pulling on a pair of pants myself," Longarm went on. "Oscar, you mind keeping an eye on this fella?"

"He ain't going nowhere," Oscar said dryly. "I reckon I can handle that chore."

Longarm climbed out of the pool and strode quickly to the dressing room he had used. He didn't bother trying to dry himself off, just stepped dripping wet into his long underwear and trousers. He took his watch with the attached derringer from the pockets of his vest and stuffed them into his pants pocket so that he wouldn't be unarmed. Then he stepped back outside to find a crowd gathering around Oscar and Ganz's corpse.

Sir Alfred Brundage was in the forefront of the group, and Longarm also saw Lady Margaret Wingate and Mark Hanley among the other guests. Most of the women shuddered and looked away at the sight of the dead man, but Lady Margaret studied the corpse with avid eyes, Longarm noted. Death didn't seem to bother her overmuch. Longarm couldn't say the same thing for Lady Margaret's companion. Hanley looked a little green, as if he might be sick at any moment.

"What the devil happened here?" demanded Sir Alfred. "Oscar, I thought you took Dr. Ganz into Trinidad this morning so that he could catch the next train."

"Yes, sir, I did," Oscar said as he nodded. "I sure don't know how he got back here and wound up, well, dead."

"Did you see him board the train?"

Oscar frowned and shook his head. "Nope. I left him at the depot and went over to the general store because Mrs. Hastings asked me to pick up a few supplies for her. I heard the train pull in while I was loadin' up the wagon, though, and then it left while I was still there. I swung back by the depot and Dr. Ganz was gone, so I figured he'd gotten on board the way he was supposed to."

"Well, clearly he didn't," Sir Alfred said testily, "or he wouldn't be here now."

Oscar rubbed his jaw. "I reckon you're right, sir."

Longarm had listened with interest to Oscar's story. He himself had not seen either Oscar or Ganz while he was in Trinidad earlier in the day. He suspected that the train had already left before he got there, since he had taken the long way around and had not been in any hurry to reach the settlement.

It seemed fairly obvious to Longarm what had happened. As soon as Oscar had left Ganz at the train station, the Prussian scientist had slipped off and probably hidden somewhere until after the train was gone. Satisfied that everyone at Briarcliff Manor thought he had left, Ganz had headed back here to the valley, still intending to somehow get his hands on the Baumhofer Cranium.

Instead, he had wound up dead. Longarm knelt beside the corpse and said, "Let's see if we can figure out what happened to him."

At first glance, the cause of Ganz's death was not apparent. Longarm checked his throat, in case he had been strangled, but there were no marks, none of the telltale bruises that almost always resulted when someone was choked to death. Longarm grasped Ganz's shoulders and got ready to roll him over.

"Wait just a moment." The words came from a surprising source: Mark Hanley. "Shouldn't we send for the sheriff and leave the body alone until he gets here?"

That was awfully civic-minded of the boy, thought Longarm. Or maybe Hanley was just familiar with the ways of badge-toters because of his own run-ins with the law. At any rate, Longarm didn't feel like waiting the hours it would take for someone to fetch Sheriff Banning from Trinidad.

"I'll take the responsibility," he said as he gripped Ganz's shoulders again, without explaining that he himself was a lawman. He rolled the dead man onto his side.

Immediately, what had happened was obvious. A narrow rent was visible in the back of Ganz's coat, and when Longarm moved it aside, he saw a matching opening in the Prussian's shirt. Beneath that was a small but ugly wound where someone had buried a knife in Ganz's back, just to the left of center. Longarm figured the blade had pierced Ganz's heart, killing him quickly, probably before there was any chance for him to make an outcry. From the look of mingled pain and surprise on Ganz's face, he hadn't been expecting the knife in the back.

"Well, now we know how he died anyway," muttered Longarm. "He was murdered."

"Murdered!" exclaimed Sir Alfred. "Good Lord. Now we have to send for the sheriff."

"I'll fetch him," Oscar offered. He hurried off toward the stable to saddle a horse, adding over his shoulder, "Ought to be back in a couple of hours."

"This is incredible," Lady Margaret said. "Who would want to murder this man? Admittedly, he's not very attractive, but that's hardly a reason to kill someone."

Hanley said, "He had that trouble with Dr. Colton over that old skull. . . ."

"Dr. Colton didn't do this," Longarm snapped as he straightened from his kneeling position beside the body.

"How do you know that?" challenged Hanley. Now that the young man had recovered from the initial shock of seeing Ganz's body, some of his natural arrogance was coming back.

I know it because her and me were romping in the pool,

thought Longarm, but he kept that to himself for two reasons. First of all, he didn't want to embarrass Emmaline, and secondly—

Secondly, he realized with a shock that what he and Emmaline had been doing didn't prove a damned thing other than that they were two healthy, lusty adults. There was no doubt in Longarm's mind that Ganz's body had been in the pool with them all along. They hadn't been able to see it because of the way the hot, spring-fed water roiled and bubbled and was murky with minerals, and it had been just luck that the currents in the pool hadn't bumped the corpse into Longarm's foot until after he and Emmaline had finished their lovemaking. So, whoever had killed Ganz had dumped the body into the pool before Longarm and Emmaline even got there.

Emmaline could have done it, Longarm realized. She could have killed Ganz, put the body in the pool, and then met Longarm on the steps later.

He didn't want to admit that she could be a killer, even to himself, but the evidence didn't rule her out. And she was still hiding in that dressing room too. Longarm glanced toward the little building, wondering why she hadn't come out once she had her clothes on. Maybe she was ashamed that she had been frolicking in the pool with him. On the other hand, nobody here at Briarcliff Manor seemed overly concerned about modesty and propriety, Emmaline included.

Longarm hadn't said anything about her being in the pool with him before Ganz's body was discovered, nor had he mentioned that she was still in the dressing room. Oscar knew, of course, because he had arrived while Emmaline was still in plain sight, but Oscar had already left for Trinidad without mentioning her. Longarm decided to keep it that way for the time being.

"You never answered my question," Mark Hanley said with a sneer, and Longarm realized all those thoughts had gone through his brain in a matter of moments.

"I know Dr. Colton didn't do this because she ain't the type to stick a knife in somebody's back," Longarm said.

"I agree," Sir Alfred put in, "but I don't suppose anyone can be eliminated as a suspect until the sheriff has had a chance to investigate." He looked down worriedly at the corpse. "We can't just leave poor Dr. Ganz lying there like that. . . ."

"I reckon we'd better not move him anymore," said Longarm.

Hanley snorted. "I thought you were the one who said he'd take the responsibility."

Longarm reined in the surge of anger he felt at the young man's attitude. "Somebody ought to fetch a blanket and cover him up," he said.

"An excellent idea," agreed Sir Alfred. "And the rest of us should go back to the house to wait for the sheriff. Someone has to keep an eye on the body, though. Mr. Parker, would you be willing to . . . ?"

"Sure," Longarm replied with a nod. "I'll stand guard."

"Why him?" demanded Hanley. "He claims he found the body. I'd say he's the most likely suspect of all."

"Well, I hadn't thought of that," admitted Sir Alfred. "But I'm certain Mr. Parker is absolutely trustworthy."

He couldn't very well explain why he felt that way, however, not without revealing Longarm's identity as a U.S. deputy marshal. Longarm didn't want that, and he communicated as much to Sir Alfred with a meaningful look.

Brundage began ushering the guests back toward the house, including the protesting Mark Hanley. Longarm went quickly into the dressing room and got his shirt, socks, and boots, pulling them on when he had returned to the side of the pool where Ganz's body lay. He waited until everyone else was back at the house and out of earshot before saying quietly, "All right, you can come out now. They're gone."

A moment later, the door of the dressing room opened and Emmaline emerged tentatively. She was fully dressed again. She said, "Thank you, Custis, for not giving me away."

"It ain't permanent, you know. Oscar saw you here with me right after we pulled Ganz's body from the pool. Once he gets back with the sheriff, the rest of the story's bound to come out."

Emmaline nodded. She carefully avoided looking at the corpse of the rival archaeologist. "I know," she said. "But I'm grateful for even that much time to . . . to pull myself together. It upset me terribly when I saw Ulrich like that. And when I thought about how he . . . he must have been in there with us the whole time. . . ."

She started to tremble, and her eyes shone with tears in the late afternoon light. Longarm stepped over to her and put his arms around her. She might be a murderer, he honestly didn't know about that, but he was fond of her anyway and didn't want to see her so upset. He patted her on the back and said, "I know."

"I . . . I had had my problems with Ulrich," she said, "but I didn't want him to come to any harm. I . . . I never hated him. I suppose for a time I even . . . loved him."

Longarm pulled back a little and frowned down at her. "Loved him?" he repeated.

Emmaline nodded. "We were engaged to be married at one time, after all."

That was news to Longarm. "When was this?" he asked.

"Oh . . ." Emmaline sniffed back some tears. "Three or four years ago. While Ulrich was a visiting professor at Harvard and I was studying at Radcliffe."

"And you two figured to get hitched?"

"Yes, but then we got into a dreadful argument and Ulrich called off the wedding and went back to Heidelberg."

"So Ganz broke the engagement?"

"That's right." Emmaline pressed her face against Longarm's chest. "I don't want to talk about this, Custis. It just makes me more upset to remember the good times when poor Ulrich is . . . is lying right over there like that."

Longarm didn't say anything, but he was busy thinking. If Ganz had snuck back here to Briarcliff Manor today and tried to steal the skull from Emmaline, that would have been reason enough itself for her to strike back at him, possibly in self-defense. With the added fact that they had been engaged several years earlier until Ganz had called off the wedding, it was reasonable to suppose that she might have been holding a grudge against him ever since then. . . .

Longarm didn't like where those thoughts were leading him, didn't like it at all.

Murder was a state crime, he told himself, not a federal one. It didn't fall under his jurisdiction. So he would only be doing his duty by staying out of this mess and letting Sheriff Banning handle it. After all, Ganz's death didn't really have anything to do with why Longarm had come here. Obadiah Jones was still his leading suspect in the attempts on Sir Alfred Brundage's life, and Jones wouldn't have had any reason to kill Ganz. Nor was it likely the preacher would have had the opportunity either, since he had probably fled back to Trinidad after his ambush of Longarm on the trail had failed.

That was assuming Jones was the one who'd bushwhacked him, Longarm reminded himself. He sighed. A fella could drive himself crazy trying to sort out all the possibilities.

Footsteps made him turn his head and look along the path that led to the house. Sir Alfred appeared, carrying a folded blanket in his arms. The Englishman stopped short at the sight of Longarm and Emmaline.

"My dear," Sir Alfred said, "what are you doing here? I noticed earlier that you weren't in the crowd, but I assumed you were in the house and hadn't heard the commotion."

Emmaline stepped away from Longarm and used the back of her hand to delicately wipe away some of the tears on her cheeks. She gave Longarm a weak smile, then said to Brundage, "Actually, I was here all along, Sir Alfred. I was with Custis when he . . . when he discovered Ulrich's body. I was in one of the dressing rooms composing myself. I was terribly upset."

"I should certainly think so." Sir Alfred turned to Longarm. "Mr. Parker, if you'll assist me, we'll cover Dr. Ganz's body."

Longarm helped him spread the blanket over the corpse. Emmaline seemed to recover even more when the body was no longer visible. She said, "I think I'd like to go back to the house now and freshen up."

"Of course," said Sir Alfred. "You go right ahead, dear. I believe I'll stay here with Mr. Parker for the moment, if you're all right to go alone. . . ."

"Certainly." Emmaline summoned up a fragile smile. "Thank you for trying to protect me, Custis."

She walked off into the gathering dusk, heading toward the house.

Brundage turned toward Longarm again. "Protect her from what?" he asked, his tone sharp. "Surely Emmaline didn't have anything to do with this dreadful crime."

"She was with me, like she said," Longarm replied heavily. "In the pool."

Understanding dawned on Sir Alfred's face. "Ah. I see. Well, at least the two of you . . . what's the word I'm looking for? . . . alibi each other."

"Not necessarily. I reckon Ganz's body had been in the pool for a while before we pulled him out."

Brundage shook his head. "I refuse to believe that Emmaline could have had anything to do with Ulrich's death. Why, she was engaged to be married to him at one time!"

"Yeah, and that's something that nobody saw fit to mention to me until now," Longarm said dryly.

"It wasn't really any of your business, was it, Marshal?"

"No, that's true enough," admitted Longarm. "I came here to find out who's been gunning for you, not to solve the murder of some German scientist."

"And what did you find out in Trinidad?"

Longarm hesitated, then said, "Reverend Jones used to

be a buffalo hunter before he became a preacher. He's still got a Sharps Big Fifty rifle, the same sort of gun that somebody used to put that slug through your window. And while I was riding back out here, somebody with a buffalo gun tried to ventilate *me*."

Sir Alfred's eyes widened. "That lunatic attempted to kill you too?"

"I can't prove it was Jones. But he knows I've been poking around. I told him I used to be a buffalo hunter, but I don't know if he believed me or not."

"I'm convinced he's responsible for all the trouble out here," Sir Alfred said vehemently. "Can't you go ahead and arrest him?"

"Not until I've asked some more questions. I want to find out if anybody saw him around town this afternoon. If they didn't, I reckon it'll be because he was out on the trail trying to put a slug through my hide."

"*Then* you'll arrest him?"

Longarm bristled a little at the way Sir Alfred was pushing him, but he supposed he understood why the Englishman was so anxious to bring the matter to a close. Nobody liked having a bushwhacker after them. But if Jones wasn't the would-be killer, it wouldn't do any good to arrest him.

Or maybe it would, Longarm suddenly thought.

"I can promise you, Sir Alfred," he said, "that if Jones doesn't have an alibi for this afternoon, he's going to wind up behind bars."

Chapter 11

After a few minutes, Sir Alfred went back to the house, leaving Longarm at the mineral baths with Ganz's body. Longarm fetched his vest from the dressing room and took out a cheroot, lighting it with a lucifer that he scratched into life. He had taken several puffs and blown a couple of nearly perfect smoke rings when footsteps made him glance toward the path with narrowed eyes.

Lady Margaret appeared there, looking fresh and even somehow innocent in a dark blue dress. Her fair hair shone, even in the dusk. Longarm was surprised to see her, and he said, "You might want to go on back to the house, ma'am. This is no place for a lady right now."

"Oh, don't worry about my delicate sensibilities, Mr. Parker," she assured him breezily. "I know all about dead men."

"Now, how would you know about that, Your Ladyship?" asked Longarm.

"My father was a brigadier in the Crimean War. I grew up listening to his tales of gore on the battlefield."

"Seeing it for yourself ain't really the same thing, though."

"I've seen dead men. I've been married twice, you know,

and widowed twice. Both of my husbands died in my presence. In my bed, as a matter of fact."

Somehow, that didn't surprise Longarm. "Older gents, were they?"

"Indeed. Older, and titled, and quite wealthy." Lady Margaret looked down at the shape under the blanket. "And there wasn't any blood on poor Dr. Ganz, I noticed."

"Nope, the pool took care of that. Washed the wound clean."

"So you see, there's no need to shoo me away as if I were about to fall into a swoon. I assure you, I shan't."

Longarm believed her. As long as she was here, he decided to go ahead and ask her a few questions.

"You didn't happen to see Ganz back around here this afternoon, did you?"

"No, Mark and I have been occupied all day." She sighed. "Though I fear he's losing his taste for our usual activities. Do you believe it? He pled fatigue and we wound up playing cards!"

"How long were you doing that?"

"For the past couple of hours—" Lady Margaret stopped abruptly and looked intently at Longarm for a second, then laughed delightedly. "You're interrogating me! You're actually questioning me as if I might have had something to do with this man's death!" She sounded amused by that prospect, rather than angry.

"Just trying to get it straight in my head what everybody's been up to today," Longarm said. "The sheriff's on his way, and he'll ask a lot more questions than I do."

"Oh, I don't mind, I assure you. Mark and I were together all morning and all afternoon. Neither one of us had the opportunity to stab Dr. Ganz. Nor would we have wanted to."

"You didn't meet Hanley until you came here, did you?"

"No."

"Then you don't really know what he might have wanted to do," Longarm pointed out. "I ain't one to gossip, but

110

I've heard that he's had some scrapes with the law before."

Lady Margaret waved a slim hand in dismissal. "Oh, those were just youthful peccadilloes." She laughed again, throatier this time. "I've been teaching him about true decadence."

Longarm bet that was true. But he wasn't expecting Lady Margaret to step closer to him and reach out to lightly rest a hand on his groin.

"I wouldn't mind getting to know you better, Mr. Parker," she said. "As I told you, poor Mark is waning in his ability to please me. Youth has its assets, but sometimes a more experienced man is just what a woman needs."

Her caress became firmer and bolder, and despite the situation, Longarm felt himself responding. As his shaft grew hard, Lady Margaret's fingers traced the length of it through his trousers, and she smiled.

"Yes, you *are* experienced, aren't you, Mr. Parker? Very experienced."

Longarm said tightly, "In case you hadn't noticed, ma'am, there's a dead man lying right there."

"I know. But *he* can't do me any good now, can he?" With that, Lady Margaret stepped closer to Longarm and brought her mouth up to his. Her lips were hot, wet, and demanding as they closed on his. Her tongue speared boldly into his mouth as she continued squeezing and caressing him.

Night was falling, and shadows were gathering in the garden and around the mineral baths. Longarm wasn't particularly worried about anybody seeing them. But he didn't like the fact that Ganz's corpse was so close by. He had already made love to Emmaline while the body was in the pool with them, but at least he hadn't known about it then. There was something to be said for ignorance.

But he couldn't ignore the situation now, so he put his hands on Lady Margaret's shoulders and gently moved her back a step. "I don't reckon we'd better be doing this," he said.

"Why in the world not? We're both adults, and if we want each other, we should indulge that desire. Otherwise, impurities will build up in our bodies and minds, and that can be quite unhealthy."

"So this is part of Sir Alfred's cleansing theory."

"Of course," she said. "Why else would I be doing this?" She gave him another squeeze.

"Because you're just about the randiest gal I ever ran into?" asked Longarm.

Lady Margaret laughed again. "You've found me out, Mr. Parker," she said. "I'm a dreadful fraud. I didn't come here for health reasons. I just like to . . ." She put her mouth close to Longarm's ear and whispered about all the things she liked to do. He felt his pulse start slugging a little harder again, and his face was warm.

"I'll keep that in mind," he said dryly.

"You do that." Lady Margaret gave him a final pat on the groin, then turned toward the house. "Come see me, Mr. Parker. Later on tonight, if you'd like."

"Don't know if I can make it," he told her honestly. "The sheriff's not here yet, and who knows how long it'll take to get things straightened out with him?"

"Well, I'll be waiting for you anyway. I hope you can see your way clear to pay me a visit."

Longarm didn't make any promises. Instead he just drew in a deep breath and blew it out in a long sigh as Lady Margaret strolled off toward the house. He waited for his pulse to slow down and the aching stiffness in his groin to go away.

It took a while.

It took a while for Oscar to get back from Trinidad with Sheriff Arch Banning too, but eventually he did. Longarm had dragged the bench out of the dressing room, and was sitting on it smoking when Banning and Sir Alfred came down from the house. Sir Alfred was carrying a lantern that cast a deceptively cheery yellow glow over the scene.

Banning looked at Longarm and grunted. "Didn't realize I'd be seeing you again today," he said.

"Neither did I," said Longarm. "No offense, Sheriff, but I'd just as soon not have had any reason to either."

"The two of you know each other then?" asked Sir Alfred.

"I stopped in at Sheriff Banning's office when I was in Trinidad," Longarm said. "Talked to him a mite about Reverend Jones and your troubles out here."

"Oh. Then he knows that you're a United States marshal."

Longarm winced. He hadn't intended for that fact to come out yet, but it was too late now. Banning was reaching over toward the blanket that was spread out over Ganz's corpse, but he stopped short and looked up as he heard Sir Alfred's comment.

"A United States marshal?" he repeated as he looked at Longarm.

"U.S. deputy marshal actually," Longarm admitted. "Working for Chief Marshal Billy Vail out of the Denver office."

Banning straightened. "I've heard of Vail. Supposed to be a good man. But I don't take it too kindly when a federal officer comes into my bailiwick and doesn't let me know what he's doing."

"Oh, dear," said Sir Alfred. "I've spoken out of turn and caused a problem."

"Nope," Longarm assured him. To Banning, he said, "My orders were to work under an alias on this assignment and keep my real identity a secret as much as possible. If that puts a burr under your saddle, Sheriff, I reckon that's just too damned bad."

For a moment, Longarm thought Banning was going to flare up at the blunt talk, but then the sheriff shrugged and said, "You had your orders. Can't hold it against a man for doing his job. Just what is your assignment, Marshal, or is that a secret too?"

"I was sent to find out who's after Sir Alfred here and put a stop to it."

"That's why you were asking around about Obadiah Jones."

"He's got a buffalo gun *and* a powerful dislike for Sir Alfred," Longarm pointed out.

Banning nodded. "Makes sense, all right."

"And somebody tried to bushwhack me this afternoon while I was on my way back out here," Longarm continued. "Whoever it was used a heavy-caliber rifle from a long distance."

"Is that so? You think it was Obadiah?"

"I wouldn't be a bit surprised. You wouldn't happen to know if he was around town after I left, would you?"

The sheriff shook his head. "I couldn't say one way or the other. But I'll ask around if you'd like."

"I'd appreciate that," Longarm said sincerely.

Banning pointed down at the body on the ground. "Now, what's all this about? Oscar told me the dead man was some German fella. One of your patients, Dr. Brundage?"

"I prefer to call them guests," said Sir Alfred, "but although Dr. Ganz did stay here last night, he was not one of the guests. In fact, he followed one of my friends and colleagues here because of a dispute he was having with her."

"Her? Who would that be?"

"Dr. Emmaline Colton, the famous archaeologist."

"I'm afraid I don't know what you're talking about," said Banning. "Arky-what?"

"It gets worse," Longarm told him. "Wait until you hear about the Baumhofer Cranium."

Between Longarm and Sir Alfred, it took only a few minutes to explain the situation to Sheriff Banning. The local lawman took off his Stetson, scrubbed a hand over his face, and shook his head as he tried to digest the details. He replaced his hat on his head and said, "Sounds pretty simple to me. Ganz must've tried to steal that old skull again, and this Dr. Colton gal stuck a knife in his back."

"I reckon it could've happened that way," said Longarm, "but Sir Alfred and I don't think Emmaline would do such a thing."

"Folks will do almost anything to protect something that's important to them," said Banning.

Longarm couldn't argue with that. He just shrugged and said, "I still don't think she did it."

"No offense, Marshal, but that's up to me to figure out. When it comes to a simple killin', that's my jurisdiction, not yours."

Longarm inclined his head in acknowledgment of that point.

"Well, let's take the body up to the house and put it in your wagon," Banning said to Sir Alfred. "I reckon you can spare Oscar to drive it into town for me?"

"Of course."

"Has this fella got any family that'd want his body sent back to Europe, or do we plant him here in Boot Hill?"

"I don't know," said Sir Alfred. "I'll have to send a wire to the University of Heidelberg and find out. I can do that first thing in the morning."

"All right. I'll have the undertaker take care of him, so he'll be ready one way or the other." Banning turned to Longarm. "Get his feet, will you?"

They hefted the corpse, and as they carried it along the winding path through the garden, Banning went on. "I'll want to ask some questions of your guests, Sir Alfred."

"Certainly. Everyone is still awake. They're disturbed by what's happened, naturally."

Oscar already had the team hitched up to the wagon, so Banning must have told him earlier that he'd be taking the body into Trinidad. Longarm and the sheriff placed the blanket-wrapped corpse on the floorboard between two of the bench seats. Banning said, "I'll tell the undertaker to send your blanket back out."

"That won't be necessary, I assure you," Sir Alfred said quickly.

"Whatever you want, Doc."

Oscar stepped up onto the wagon box, and Banning waved him on. Flapping the reins, Oscar got the team moving. The wagon rolled away into the night.

"Now," Banning said as he turned toward the house, "let's see about those questions."

Banning didn't want any company while he talked to the guests, so Longarm headed for the kitchen to finally satisfy the hunger that had been gnawing at him for hours.

Mrs. Hastings, the cook, was still there, having fed the rest of the guests their dinner a short time earlier. Longarm lifted the lid of a pot that was staying warm on the stove and wrinkled his nose as he leaned over it to sniff.

" 'Tis stew," Mrs. Hastings told him.

"What kind?"

She just frowned ominously and shook her head. "Ye don't want to know."

He stepped closer to her and lowered his voice to ask, "You wouldn't happen to have anything else around here to eat, would you, Mrs. Hastings?"

"Well . . ." She glanced around nervously, then beckoned for Longarm to come closer. "Dinna ye tell anyone," she whispered, "but I've got a chunk o' roast beef left over from the supper I took down to Oscar and Jed. Ye're welcome to it if ye want it."

Impulsively, Longarm threw his arms around the woman and gave her a hug. "If I want it?" he said. "Mrs. Hastings, right now you're about the prettiest gal I've ever seen."

She pushed out of his embrace and gathered up her apron to swat at him with it. "Go on with ye now! Sit down at the table, an' I'll bring the roast from the pantry. Got a piece o' apple pie left over too."

"Reckon I must've died and gone to heaven," Longarm said.

116

"Don't be jokin' about such things," Mrs. Hastings told him with a frown. She went into the pantry that adjoined the kitchen, and came back a few moments later with a plate containing a thick slab of roast beef and a carving knife. She was also carrying a saucer with the piece of pie on it.

Longarm dug in, using the fork Mrs. Hastings placed on the table. Between bites that he hacked off the roast with the carving knife, he asked, "Religious woman, are you, Mrs. Hastings?"

"Of course I am."

"You wouldn't happen to go to Reverend Jones's church in Trinidad, would you?"

"A good Irish woman like meself? No, I go to Mass as the mission."

"Reverend Jones thinks the things that go on out here are sinful," said Longarm. "He even calls this the valley of sin. You don't feel the same way?"

"I don't necessarily approve of all the carryin'-on," Mrs. Hastings replied with a frown, "but the real sin is the way Sir Alfred makes his guests eat all those things that I wouldn't hardly even consider food." She sniffed in disdain. "But then, what more can ye expect from an Englishman?"

Longarm recalled that the English and the Irish didn't always get along too well, at least over there in their home countries. Here in the American West, such things didn't seem to matter as much.

"You know Reverend Jones, though, don't you?" Longarm persisted.

"Everybody around these parts knows the reverend. There are those who swear by him. And then there are those who swear *at* him. From what I've heard, he's a bit touched in the head."

"Could be." Longarm chewed and swallowed the last bite of roast, then pushed the empty plate aside and pulled the saucer of pie in front of him. He took a bite and closed his

117

eyes, letting out a tiny moan of pleasure. When he had swallowed, he said, "That's mighty good pie."

"Ye're lucky there was any left over. Usually Oscar and Jed polish off everything I take 'em."

"They seem like good fellas," Longarm said, just making conversation as he ate.

"Oh, aye, the salt o' the earth, those two are. The only ones left from the old ranch crew. An' me, of course. I cooked for the hands."

"Is that so?" asked Longarm, growing more interested. He hadn't heard much about the history of this place before Sir Alfred took it over. "Who owned the spread?"

"A syndicate back in England. I suppose that's how Sir Alfred got his hands on it. The owners eventually decided to sell, even though the ranch was makin' a bit of profit. Just too far away, I reckon."

"They must've had somebody ramrodding the operation."

"Oh, sure, Oscar was the foreman and ranch manager. Did a fine job too."

"But he stayed on anyway, once Sir Alfred bought the place?"

"Aye. And Jed stayed on too. What with him bein' so stove up and all, it would've been hard for him to get a job somewheres else. I reckon Oscar just likes it here. He could've ridden for some other spread."

"Folks get set in their ways and don't want to start over sometimes," Longarm commented.

Mrs. Hastings nodded. "That's one reason I'm still here. An' to tell the truth, I like a lot of the guests." She laughed. "It's downright entertainin' sometimes, the way they carry on with all their antics. O' course, 'tis indecent, but still . . ."

Longarm scraped the last bit of pie from the saucer and sat back, not really satisfied but feeling a lot better now than he had before eating. "I don't know how long I'm going to be here," he said, "but I'd surely like it if I could get some more food like this."

Mrs. Hastings wagged a finger at him. "Just be careful that Sir Alfred don't find out. He wouldn't take it kindly if he knew I was feedin' one of the guests things he considers to be unhealthy."

Longarm picked up the carving knife and toyed with it idly. "Well, maybe those fellas are on to something when they say a gent'd live longer if he gave up smoking and drinking and eating everything that tastes good." He grinned and laid the knife aside. "Me, I reckon I'd rather live dangerously."

Chapter 12

Several hours passed before Longarm met with Sheriff Banning and Sir Alfred in the book-lined study. That was where Banning had been questioning the guests, and the sheriff had a frustrated expression on his face as he leaned back in the chair behind Sir Alfred's desk.

"This bunch doesn't know anything except that they want to get back to their tomcatting," Banning declared.

Sir Alfred was standing by the shelves, his hands clasped together behind his back. Longarm sat down in the chair in front of the desk and said, "Nobody knew anything about Ganz's murder?"

"Nobody would even admit to seeing him around the place today," said Banning. "It's like nobody laid eyes on him from the time he left this morning until you pulled him out of that mineral bath, Parker."

"Actually, the name's Long. Custis Long."

Banning grunted. "Whatever you call yourself is all right with me. I just wish I knew what to do about this murder. Usually when somebody gets killed around these parts, it's because they got in an argument with somebody else and got themselves ventilated during the discussion. Or else some owlhoot gets an itchy trigger finger and shoots somebody while he's robbing a stagecoach or holding up a bank.

A case like this, with a prehistoric skull and a bunch of rich folks cavorting with each other . . ." He shook his head. "I just don't know what to make of it."

"I reckon Dr. Colton claimed she hadn't seen Ganz since this morning?" asked Longarm.

"That's right. She was pretty upset, but I suppose that's natural enough, seeing as how she used to be engaged to the gent but now they are rivals."

"And bitter ones, at that," Sir Alfred put in.

Longarm frowned. Comments like that didn't help matters a bit. In fact, it just made it sound as if Emmaline had even more reason for wanting Ganz dead. Of course, there was some truth to that. . . .

"But I don't know hardly when she would have had time to kill anybody," Banning went on. "She was around where folks could see her most of the day. It doesn't take much time to stick a knife in somebody's back, but whoever killed Ganz had to drag him to that pool and dump him in too. I went back out there with the lantern and took another look around. Didn't see any blood, so I reckon it's safe to say Ganz was killed somewhere else and then brought there."

Longarm leaned forward. "Here's a question for you: How'd Ganz get back out here in the first place? He couldn't have walked all the way from Trinidad."

"Say, that's right," Banning said, some eagerness coming back into his voice. "He must've rented a horse somewhere. I'll ask around at the livery stables first thing in the morning. Wherever he got the horse, maybe he said something to somebody about what he was planning to do."

Longarm thought that was pretty unlikely, considering Ganz's superior attitude, but he supposed it wouldn't hurt to check. That would be one more loose end tied up, even if it didn't lead anywhere.

Banning pushed back his chair and stood up. "I'll ask about Reverend Jones too," he said to Longarm. "I haven't forgotten about that. But I got to admit, Long, I'm more interested in finding out who killed Ganz than I am in handling your case for you."

"I can ask the questions, if that's what you want," said Longarm, a little irritated at Banning's tone.

"No, that's all right. I got to be nosing around anyway." The sheriff nodded to Sir Alfred. "Good night, Doc."

"Good night, Sheriff."

Banning hesitated before he left the study. "Better keep your eyes and ears open," he advised. "Could be whoever stuck that knife in Ganz ain't finished yet."

Sir Alfred's eyes widened. "Oh, dear Lord. I hadn't thought of that."

Longarm had, though he didn't think there was any real danger of the killer striking again tonight.

Banning went out, and Sir Alfred resumed his normal chair behind the desk. "This is awful," he said with a sigh. "First there were those attempts on my life, and now someone else has been murdered here at Briarcliff Manor. Things were going so well for a while. Why did all this trouble have to start?"

Longarm started to reach for a cheroot, then stopped as he remembered how Sir Alfred felt about smoking. Instead he asked, "What made you decide to come to Colorado in the first place?"

"Primarily, it was the air that attracted me," replied Sir Alfred. "I visited here several years ago and was struck by how clean and healthful the atmosphere is, especially at this altitude. Haven't you ever noticed it?"

"Can't say as I have," Longarm replied honestly. "But then, I've ridden plenty of high country trails, so I reckon I must be used to it."

"I daresay you're correct. At any rate, I was acquainted with Lord Aubrey St. Clair, the head of the syndicate that owned this property, and when he mentioned that he and his partners wished to sell it, I jumped at the chance."

"If you don't mind my asking, where'd you come up with enough money to buy a working cattle ranch?"

Sir Alfred smiled. "My sanitarium in England was quite successful. I moved here simply because I wanted to, rather than because of any failure in England."

"What about all the cattle?"

"I had Oscar handle the sale of them, which also added to the financial stability of Briarcliff Manor."

"I think I would have hung on to the stock and kept the ranch operation going too," Longarm commented.

"I considered it, but in the end I decided it would be better to devote all of my time and energy to achieving cures for all the ills of my guests."

Longarm nodded slowly. "And for a while, everything went all right."

"Yes." Sir Alfred's normally mild face hardened. "Until that horrible man Jones took it into his head to ruin me. I wish now I never hired poor Alice."

"Poor Alice?"

"Well, yes. Can you imagine living with a man such as the Reverend Jones?"

Longarm couldn't, and he said as much. Sir Alfred went on. "I took pity on the girl, I suppose, but she paid me back by telling her father about what goes on here, and that started all the problems."

"Well, I'll do my best to put a stop to them," Longarm assured him. "If Jones doesn't have an alibi for this afternoon, I'm going to go ahead and arrest him."

"A capital idea, Marshal. Would you like a drink?"

The question took Longarm by surprise. "A shot of Maryland rye would go down right nice," he said without thinking.

Sir Alfred looked appalled. "Oh, no, I was referring to a glass of my special vegetable essence. It's just the thing to help a person get a good night's sleep."

Longarm figured if he drank some of that vile stuff before going to bed, he'd be up all night hurrying to the facilities. He managed to put a smile on his face as he said, "No, thanks. I reckon I'll just go ahead and turn in."

"Well, then, I'll bid you good night." Sir Alfred sighed wearily. "Let us hope that tomorrow will be better."

As long as nobody else got killed, it would be, thought Longarm.

He was halfway expecting to find Emmaline or Lady Margaret waiting for him in his room, but it was empty when he got there. He supposed Emmaline was probably so wrung out by everything that had happened that she had gone to sleep. And maybe Mark Hanley had gotten a second wind and was keeping Lady Margaret occupied.

Longarm undressed and stretched out in bed after blowing out the lamp. He stared up at the dark ceiling and frowned in thought. Something was bothering him, roaming around in the back of his mind, but he couldn't dab a loop on it. He figured worrying about it would keep him awake, but instead he dozed off almost right away, falling into a sound sleep that wasn't disturbed until the next morning when the bright sunlight slanting through a gap in the curtains over the window woke him.

The water in the basin was cold, but he used it to wash up and shave anyway, then dressed in a fresh shirt and his brown tweed suit and went downstairs, leaving his Stetson in the room. About half the guests were still eating breakfast in the dining room, Lady Margaret and Mark Hanley among them. Hanley grinned unpleasantly at Longarm and said, "Find any more bodies since last night, Parker?"

"Nope," Longarm answered curtly as he sat down at the table. "Hope I don't."

"Ganz didn't strike me as any great loss," Hanley said breezily. "He seemed rather arrogant."

Talk about the pot calling the kettle black, thought Longarm. There was some truth to those old sayings, or else they wouldn't have been repeated enough to become commonplace.

"I didn't see you again after our visit at the mineral baths," Lady Margaret said to Longarm, prompting a frown from Hanley. Obviously, he hadn't known that she had gone back down there to talk to Longarm, and he didn't much care for the idea either.

That was probably just what Lady Margaret had in mind, Longarm told himself. If she could make Hanley jealous, maybe he would show even more attention to her. And she was the kind of woman who could never get enough male attention. Longarm had already discovered that for himself.

He said, "I had to talk to the sheriff, and then I was so tuckered out that I just went on to bed."

"By yourself?" Lady Margaret asked with a wicked smile.

"Sleeping was all I had in mind."

"Such a waste."

Hanley leaned forward, asking brusquely, "Has the sheriff figured out who killed Ganz?"

Longarm shook his head. "Not that I know of."

"So, what are you going to do today?" Hanley asked.

"I've got to ride into Trinidad," Longarm replied honestly. "Got a few errands to run, and I need to send a wire."

He'd been trying to dodge Hanley's question, but come to think of it, he *did* need to send a telegram. An idea had popped suddenly into his head, and he wanted to check it out.

"Such a shame," said Hanley, but he didn't sound as if he meant it. "I know Margaret here was looking forward to getting to know you better." The words had a vicious edge to them.

"Well, I shall just have to muddle along with your company, shan't I?" she shot back at him. Hanley glowered.

Mrs. Hastings came out of the kitchen and put a bowl of mush in front of Longarm. She dropped an eyelid in a wink at him that none of the others could see. Longarm spooned up some of the stuff and tasted it, and he was surprised by the crunch and the unmistakable taste of bacon. Mrs. Hastings had slipped some real food into the mush for him.

The other guests finished their meals and left the dining

room as Longarm lingered over his food until he was the only one left at the table. Mrs. Hastings brought a cup from the kitchen and set it next to him. The aroma drifting up from the dark liquid was just as distinctive as the taste of bacon.

"Arbuckle's," she whispered. "With eggshells ground up in it."

"Bless your heart," Longarm said fervently. He drank the coffee quickly, knowing that Sir Alfred would be offended if he caught him imbibing the illicit brew. The only thing that could have made it better was a dollop of Tom Moore, but Longarm was grateful for what he could get.

Sure enough, Sir Alfred Brundage came into the dining room only moments after Mrs. Hastings had taken away Longarm's bowl and cup. "Ah, there you are," Sir Alfred said. "Did you sleep well, Mr. Parker?"

"Yep," replied Longarm. "Sort of surprised me too."

"I'm afraid my slumber was not so restful. I kept thinking about everything that has happened."

"No need to dwell on the past," Longarm told him. "I'm going to clear up this business with the preacher, and I reckon Sheriff Banning will get to the bottom of Ganz's murder."

He wasn't as confident as he sounded about that last part. Banning struck him as an honest lawman, but not particularly bright.

Longarm stood up. "I'm riding into Trinidad; be back about the middle of the day, I hope."

"Please be careful."

Longarm knew what Sir Alfred meant. That bushwhacker was still out there somewhere.

He got his hat from his room, then went to the stable and had Jed saddle the same lineback dun for him that he had ridden the day before. The old hostler smacked his lips over toothless gums and said, "Oscar's been tellin' me about how that foreign feller got hisself killed. You heard anything about who might've done it?"

Longarm shook his head. "Afraid not."

Jed frowned worriedly and said, "I don't like killin's. A feller who'll kill once is liable to do it again."

"I reckon that's true. But you shouldn't have anything to worry about, old-timer. You're not a threat to anybody."

Jed shrugged and went on saddling the dun. He was still frowning when Longarm swung up into the saddle and rode away.

He took the main road to Trinidad this time, rather than following the roundabout trail from the far end of the valley. His instincts told him that this case was drawing to a close, that soon there would no longer be any reason to conceal his true identity.

Nobody tried to bushwhack him this time, and he reached Trinidad in less than an hour. His first stop was the Western Union office, where he used a stub of a pencil to scrawl out a message to Billy Vail asking Vail to check the records at the Colorado Livestock Exchange. He paid for the telegram and told the clerk he'd be around town for a while if a reply came in. Otherwise, the clerk was to hold the reply until Longarm called for it.

From the Western Union office, Longarm strolled down the boardwalk to the sheriff's office and jail. Banning was standing out front, his hands tucked in the pockets of his denim trousers as he surveyed the street. He grunted a greeting as Longarm came up to him.

"Any luck on finding out how Ganz got back out to Briarcliff Manor?" asked Longarm.

"Oh, sure," replied Banning. "It wasn't hard to find out. He rented a horse, just like we thought he must've. Got it down at the Wilcox Livery."

"Horse come back in on its own?"

Banning shook his head. "No, and Wilcox ain't happy about that either. It's starting to look like whoever killed Ganz stole the horse too."

"One more reason to hang the son of a bitch," commented Longarm as he took a cheroot from his vest pocket.

He offered the smoke to Banning, who shook his head.

"I prefer a pipe," he said.

Longarm lit the cheroot, then asked, "You got a description of the horse?"

"Chestnut mare with a white blaze on its face."

Longarm nodded. "I'll keep my eyes open for it. Now, what about Reverend Jones?"

"I haven't talked to everybody in town, mind you, but I haven't found anybody who saw him around here yesterday afternoon."

"That's good enough for me."

Banning looked at Longarm in surprise. "What do you mean?"

"I mean I'm going to arrest that bushwhacking, back-shooting preacher," Longarm declared.

"Now, hold on just a damned minute," Banning said sharply. "You don't have any proof that Obadiah ambushed anybody, let alone caused any of that other trouble out at Brundage's place."

"He's got a reason to hate Brundage—or at least he thinks so—and he's got a Sharps Big Fifty and no alibi for yesterday afternoon." Longarm's face was grim. "That's enough for me." He started to turn away.

Banning's hand shot out and gripped Longarm's arm. "You can't—"

"The hell I can't," Longarm said coldly. "This is a federal matter, Sheriff, since Sir Alfred is a foreign citizen who requested the aid of the United States government. Now, I'll thank you to let go of my arm."

With an angry glare, Banning released Longarm. "You're making a mistake," he said.

"I don't think so. And if I am, it's my mistake to make."

Banning couldn't argue with that, but Longarm felt the sheriff's eyes boring into his back as he walked along the street toward the church. He hoped he would find Jones there so that he could get this over with.

Longarm opened the door of the church and stepped inside, hearing music from the old piano as he did so. Alice was sitting on the piano bench, her fingers moving over the keys. She was playing a hymn, concentrating on the music so that she didn't even notice that Longarm had come in. He recognized the tune as "Amazing Grace" as he started up the aisle toward the front of the church.

The door to the rear of the building opened and Obadiah Jones came out, stopping short when he saw Longarm striding toward him. The music came to an abrupt halt as well when Alice finally noticed that Longarm was there.

"Reverend Jones," Longarm said in a loud, clear voice, "I'm United States Deputy Marshal Custis Long, and you're under arrest."

"Arrest?" exclaimed Jones. "What for?"

"No!" Alice cried as she came to her feet.

"For the attempted murder of Sir Alfred Brundage, an English citizen," said Longarm.

Jones's lip curled at the mention of Sir Alfred. "I never tried to harm the man," he said. "Hate the sin but love the sinner, that's what the Good Book says."

"But you hate Sir Alfred anyway, don't you?" Longarm prodded. "You said he was nothing but a minion of Satan, and it's your job to fight Satan and everybody who backs his play."

"You've lost your mind," sneered Jones. "I'll pray for you."

"Better pray for yourself," Longarm advised. He slipped the .44 derringer out of his vest pocket and eared back the hammer. "Come on, preacher. It's time you were behind bars where you belong."

"No!" Alice shouted again, and this time, she did something about it. Longarm saw the movement from the corner of his eye as she snatched up the hymnal from the piano and flung it at him.

Longarm wasn't expecting that, and as he started to turn toward Alice, the heavy book smacked into the wrist of his gun hand and knocked it aside. Jones jumped him at the same time, lashing out and hitting Longarm's wrist with the edge of his left hand. That drove the barrels of the derringer toward the floor, and Longarm's hand went numb from the blow for a second, so that the little weapon slipped from his fingers.

This wasn't going right at all, thought Longarm. He blocked a punch that Jones swung at his head, then struck a blow of his own, a short left jab that caught the preacher in the face. The feeling was coming back into Longarm's right hand now, so he clenched it into a fist and drove it into Jones's midsection.

Alice was coming at him, but Longarm didn't give her a chance to jump on his back this time. He put a hand out, planted it between her breasts, and shoved. She stumbled backward, losing her balance and sitting down hard on one of the pews. Longarm swung back toward Jones as one of the reverend's fists grazed the side of his head, causing pain to shoot through his ear. Longarm grimaced, parried the next blow, then stepped in and smashed a combination into Jones, the left catching the preacher in the solar plexus, the right whistling up in an uppercut that landed solidly on Jones's jaw. Jones came up off the floor and went over backward, landing heavily. He rolled onto his side and lay there groggily, evidently with all the fight gone out of him.

The doors of the church banged open behind Longarm. "That's enough!" Sheriff Banning shouted. Longarm glanced over his shoulder and saw the local lawman stalking toward him.

"You're right, Sheriff, it's enough," Longarm said as he massaged his aching right fist with his left hand. "Jones fought back when I tried to arrest him, so there's your proof he's guilty."

"That doesn't prove anything except that he's a hot-headed fool," snapped Banning.

"Not in my book," Longarm insisted. "I reckon Uncle Sam and I can count on you to haul him down and lock him up in your jail until I can make arrangements to take him back to Denver?"

The line of Banning's jaw was tight and angry as he said, "I don't have much choice, do I?"

"Not a bit," agreed Longarm. "Not unless you want to go up against the federal government."

"You're a heavy-handed son of a bitch, you know that?"

Longarm swallowed his own anger as he bent to pick up his derringer and replace it in his vest pocket. "Just doing my job, Sheriff," he said. "Why don't you do yours?"

"You're wrong," Alice said miserably from the pew where she was still sitting. "My pa wouldn't really hurt anybody. He wouldn't."

Longarm ignored her and said, "Well, Sheriff?"

Banning grimaced and reached down to grasp Jones's collar. He hauled the preacher to his feet and said, "Come on, Obadiah. I reckon you're under arrest." He led the stumbling Jones out of the church and turned toward the jail.

"I hope you're proud of yourself," Alice snarled at Longarm as he brushed off his suit.

"Just doing my job, Miss Jones," he said.

But as he turned to walk out of the church, he wished he felt a little bit better about it too.

Chapter 13

Longarm left the church and went by the jail to make sure that Sheriff Banning had Obadiah Jones locked up safely. The preacher was behind bars, all right. The cell block door was open, and Longarm could hear Jones's voice coming from beyond it. Jones was praying in a loud voice.

Banning glared at Longarm from the desk. "I've done your dirty work for you, Marshal," he said. "Anything else you need?"

"Seems to me you'd be glad to get a bushwhacker locked up," Longarm said.

"I'm still not convinced Obadiah's your man. You're putting an awful lot of weight behind the fact that nobody saw him around yesterday afternoon while somebody was shooting at you."

"Question him yourself. See if he'll admit where he was."

Banning rubbed his jaw. "I might just do that," he said.

That was all right with Longarm, as long as Jones stayed locked up in the jail. He gave the sheriff a curt nod, then walked on down the street to the Western Union office.

"Oh, it's you again, Mr. Parker," the young clerk said. "I got your reply from Denver for you." He slid a yellow message form under the bars that formed the window of his cage behind the counter.

Longarm picked up the flimsy. The message was short and to the point: *3984 STOP VAIL.* Longarm smiled a little. His hunch was still a long way from paying off, but at least he had something to work with now.

He flipped a coin to the clerk and left the telegraph office, returning to the hitch rack where he had tied the dun. His business in Trinidad was finished, at least for the time being.

The ride back out to Briarcliff Manor was peaceful. It was a beautiful day, and under other circumstances, Longarm was sure he would have enjoyed it. As it was, his head was still too full of all the strange goings-on for him to get much pleasure out of his surroundings.

He circled the manor house and rode to the stable, where he found Jed and Oscar engaged in a game of checkers. They looked up at him, and evidently Oscar noticed the expression on Longarm's face. "Somethin' wrong, Mr. Parker?" he asked.

"The name's Long, U.S. Deputy Marshal Custis Long." It was time to end this masquerade, since it no longer served any purpose. "I've just arrested Reverend Jones for trying to murder your boss."

Both Oscar and Jed stared at him, thunderstruck. Finally, Jed found his voice and asked in disbelieving tones, "What? That preacher from Trinidad? He's been tryin' to kill Sir Alfred?"

"That's right," said Longarm as he stepped down from the saddle. "Sir Alfred's kept it quiet, but there have been several attempts on his life lately. He asked for help from the government, and I got the job of sorting things out. Jones is behind bars now, where he belongs."

Oscar let out a low whistle. "Damn, I wouldn't hardly have believed it. Sure, Jones is downright annoyin', but a killer?"

"Would-be killer," Longarm corrected. "It's just luck he

wasn't successful when he tried to bushwhack your boss—and me."

"He came after you too?" asked Jed.

Longarm nodded. "Once he'd figured out I wasn't really who I claimed to be. He must've realized I was a lawman of some sort."

"A marshal, you say?"

"That's right."

"Well," Oscar said slowly, "I got to admit you didn't seem like no hardware salesman I ever met, Mr. Parker. Or Long, was it?"

"That's right. Custis Long."

"The one they sometimes call Longarm?"

The big lawman grimaced slightly. He'd never set out to make a reputation for himself, just to do his job. But he nodded and said, "Yeah."

"What are you goin' to do now?" asked Jed.

"Tell Sir Alfred he can stop worrying. Then I reckon tomorrow I'll catch the train to Denver and take Jones along with me to the federal lockup until he can stand trial."

Oscar stood up and extended his hand. "I'd like to shake with you, Marshal. Sounds like you've saved the boss from a heap of trouble."

"That's what I set out to do," Longarm said as he shook with Oscar. Then he left the two men to return to their checker game once Jed had unsaddled and rubbed down the dun.

The mineral baths were in use again. Longarm could hear laughing and squealing coming from them as he skirted the garden. At least some of the guests must have gotten over any squeamishness they felt about a dead man being found in one of the pools. Or maybe they were just avoiding that particular one.

He went inside and headed straight for Sir Alfred's study, hoping he would find the Englishman there. Before he could reach it, however, Emmaline came out of one of the massage rooms with a huge, fluffy white towel wrapped around her. Her shoulders were bare, and Longarm suspected she wasn't wearing anything underneath that towel.

"Custis!" she exclaimed. "You have a bad habit of disappearing. Didn't you come here to relax?"

"Nope, not really," Longarm told her. "I've been working ever since I got here."

"Working?" she repeated. "Working on what?"

"Trying to find out who's been trying to kill Sir Alfred." Emmaline's eyes began to widen.

"You see," Longarm went on, "I'm really a U.S. deputy marshal."

"I don't believe it," Emmaline said. "You're a lawman?"

"Yep. I'd show you my badge and bona fides, but I left 'em in Denver on account of I was supposed to work in secret on this job. But it's over now, so it don't really matter anymore."

"Over?"

He nodded. "I arrested Reverend Jones a little while ago and had him locked up in the Trinidad jail."

"This is an incredible story." Emmaline frowned at him. "I suppose I should be angry at you for lying to me all along."

Longarm shrugged. "I never meant to cause any trouble for you, Emmaline. It just sort of worked out that I couldn't tell you who I really am until now."

"Well, at least it's all over, and now maybe you *can* relax, at least until you have to start back to Denver." She moved a step closer to him, close enough to rest a hand on his chest. "Come in here with me. I'll give you a massage."

"I'd like to," Longarm replied honestly, "but I've got to find Sir Alfred and fill him in on what's happened."

She had the good graces to look disappointed. "Oh, all right. He was in one of the cleansing rooms earlier, but I don't know where he is now."

"I'll find him," Longarm told her. "Don't worry about that."

She came up on her toes and gave him a peck on the

cheek. "Come see me later," she ordered him in a husky whisper.

"I'll try," he said.

She started down the hall toward the stairs, giving him an enticing look over her shoulder as she did so. It was hard for Longarm not to follow her.

She was wrong about one thing, however. It wasn't all over. There was still the matter of Ulrich Ganz's murder, and even though it might not be Longarm's job to get to the bottom of that crime, he had a feeling he wasn't through with that part of it yet.

He went on to the study, knocked, and heard Sir Alfred's voice from inside tell him to come in. The Englishman was at his desk when Longarm entered the room. "Ah, Mr. Parker," he said.

"No need for that anymore," Longarm told him. "You might as well start using my real handle. I reckon it won't be long until everybody in Trinidad knows who I really am, and that goes for out here too."

"You mean you're no longer working incognito?" Sir Alfred asked in surprise.

"Didn't seem like there was any need for it," replied Longarm with a shrug. "Reverend Jones is behind bars. I'll be taking him back to Denver tomorrow. You can rest easy, Sir Alfred."

Brundage leaned back in his chair with a sigh. "Thank heavens," he said. "You don't know what a strain it's been, knowing that somewhere out there was someone who wanted me dead."

"I can imagine," Longarm said dryly.

"I'm sure you can. In your line of work, you must have made many enemies."

"More'n a few," admitted Longarm.

"I take it you spoke to Sheriff Banning?"

"He's the one who locked up Jones for me."

"Has he made any progress on solving Ulrich's murder?"

Longarm shook his head. "Not really."

"So, that's still troublesome," Sir Alfred said with a frown. "I wish things would just get back to normal."

Longarm didn't say anything, but for him, folks dying around him while he tried to untangle a mess of motives and opportunity sort of *was* normal.

Sir Alfred stood up and extended his hand across the desk. "Thank you, Marshal," he said. "I can assure you, I shall be writing a glowing letter of praise to your superior about your handling of this case."

"No need for that," Longarm told him as they shook hands.

"Please, no false modesty on your part. You seized on the culprit almost immediately, and you risked your own life to bring him to justice."

Such talk made Longarm uncomfortable. He said, "Well, I'll be seeing you around. I reckon it's all right for me to stay here one more night?"

"Certainly. Stay as long as you like."

"Much obliged."

That much was the truth. Longarm wasn't ready to say good-bye to Emmaline just yet.

He ate lunch with the other guests, all of whom were buzzing about the fact that he was really a federal lawman. The word had certainly gotten around fast. He had belted on the cross-draw rig with the holstered Colt, since there was no longer any need to pretend to be something he wasn't, and the weight of the gun on his hip felt damned good. A man got used to such things, and missed them when they weren't there.

"A federal man, eh?" Mark Hanley said, trying not to show that he was impressed. "Perhaps you know my father, Senator Hanley?"

"Never had the pleasure," said Longarm, "but I've heard of him plenty of times." He didn't add that one minor reason he had come to Briarcliff Manor was to keep young Hanley from getting into any more trouble and embarrassing his politician father. So far, Hanley seemed to be on his best behavior, if you didn't count the fact that he was bedding a beautiful English noblewoman who was several years older than he was.

Emmaline was sitting next to Longarm, and her hand kept straying over to his thigh during the meal. He tried not to let any reaction show on his face, even when she ventured still further and stroked her fingers over the buttons of his fly.

The food was green and leafy for the most part, and Longarm felt like a rabbit nibbling on it. He was still hungry when the meal was over, but his plans to sneak into the kitchen later on and get some proper fare from Mrs. Hastings were forestalled by his newfound celebrity. All afternoon long, there were guests talking to him, asking him questions about the case that had brought him there and the work that he did, until he wished they would all go back to their romping and leave him alone. Surely lovemaking was more interesting than talking to a lawman.

Supper was a little more filling but no less frustrating. Still, the other guests' interest in Longarm seemed to be fading slightly, and he was grateful for that. He supposed that with the fall of darkness, their thoughts were turning back to the real reasons they had come to Briarcliff Manor.

After dinner, some of the guests went off to the cleansing rooms, and Sir Alfred accompanied them to supervise the procedures. Longarm headed for the study, but Emmaline caught him on the way.

"Aren't you coming upstairs, Custis?" she asked as she stroked his arms and leaned close to him.

"In a little while," he promised her. "There's something I have to do first."

"Well," she said with a seductive smile, "don't be too long about it. I might get bored and start without you."

The thought of that made tiny beads of sweat pop out on Longarm's forehead, but he forced the mental image out of his brain. "Just give me a little while," he said again.

Emmaline finally agreed and headed upstairs, and for the first time all day, Longarm found himself alone. Grateful for that, he hurried to Sir Alfred's study, hoping the door wouldn't be locked.

It wasn't, and as Longarm slipped inside the room, he saw that the lamp on the desk was burning. Sir Alfred probably wouldn't be gone long, so Longarm knew he had to hurry. When he had been in there earlier in the day, he had looked around unobtrusively and spotted what he wanted on one of the smaller shelves behind the desk. He went straight to the shelf now and pulled a small leather-bound book from it. A piece of twine was tied around it. He untied the twine and opened the book, quickly scanning the columns of dates and numbers written inside it. The latest date was some seven months earlier, and the number beside it was 7,817.

Longarm grunted in satisfaction and snapped the book shut. That just about did it. He retied the twine around the slender little volume and replaced it on the shelf. Then he went to the door and listened intently for a moment before opening it. The corridor outside was deserted, as he had thought. He eased the study door shut and headed for the stairs.

He stopped short when he reached the door of his room. Out of long habit, he had left a match stick wedged between the door and the jamb, about six inches above the floor. It was gone now, indicating that somebody had been in his room since he'd been there earlier in the afternoon to collect his Colt.

That didn't necessarily mean trouble, he thought as he glanced from his door to the one across the hall. He had supposed that Emmaline would be waiting for him in her room, but maybe she had decided to slip into his instead. She might be in there now, stretched out nude between the sheets of his bed, ready for him to join her.

There was only one way to find out, he told himself. He grasped the doorknob with his left hand and twisted it. He went in fast, his right hand on the butt of his gun.

"Oh, my," Lady Margaret Wingate said from the bed. "You have a gun *and* you're glad to see me."

Longarm took a deep breath. "Ma'am, what are you doing here?"

"Isn't it obvious?" Lady Margaret asked with a smile.

Longarm supposed it was. Even though he had expected another woman to be naked in his bed, Lady Margaret was here for the same reason as he had thought Emmaline would be. She was sitting up, propped against some pillows behind her, and there was a heavy-lidded look to her eyes. Her bare breasts, crowned with large brown nipples, heaved slightly. The sheet was pulled to her waist, but as Longarm watched, she threw it aside and spread her legs a little so that he could see the tender pink folds of her femininity nestled in the downy blond thatch.

"I've been waiting for you for what seems like forever, Custis," she said. "Now, please—and I don't say that often—come over here and make love to me."

Longarm cast one more glance over his shoulder toward Emmaline's door, then did something that he hoped he wouldn't regret later.

He closed his own door and started walking toward the bed.

Longarm could understand why Mark Hanley was worn out. Lady Margaret had the appetites of two or three normal women. She had started by stripping all his clothes off him, then kneeling before him to engulf his shaft with her mouth. He was rock-hard by that time, and he was amazed at how much of the fleshy pole the blond woman was able to swallow. He thought several times that he was about to erupt in her mouth, but not surprisingly, she knew all the tricks of how to hold off a man's climax. When she had continued the French lesson far longer than he ever would have dreamed possible, she finally released him and sprawled out on the bed, rolling over on her stomach.

That was all right with Longarm. He enjoyed taking a woman from behind, standing beside the bed and driving into her while she knelt on all fours. . . .

But that wasn't what Lady Margaret had in mind. He had never considered himself a prude—far from it, in fact—but he was still a mite surprised when she reached under the covers and produced a short whip similar to the quirt that a bronco buster might use.

"Here," she said, holding it back toward him. "Take this and use it on me."

"Damn it," he exclaimed. "I can't do that!"

She twisted around and looked up at him imploringly. "Custis, you have to. I . . . I need this. I need it so badly you can't possibly know."

"But this ain't the sort of thing I usually do. . . ."

She forced the whip into his hand. "For me, Custis," she whispered. "I promise you, you won't regret it."

Longarm wasn't so sure about that. He stood there beside the bed, nude and feeling more than a little foolish as he looked down at the whip in his hand. This was what he got, he supposed, for not going straight to Emmaline's room.

Lady Margaret rolled over on her belly again and started to writhe back and forth. "Punish me, Custis," she gasped. "Now, my darling, hurry! And don't spare the lash!"

Longarm hesitated.

"Please, Custis. Don't make me wait any longer!"

Tentatively, Longarm raised the whip, wondering how in the hell he got himself in messes like this one.

That was when a soft knock sounded on the door, and Emmaline Colton's voice called quietly, "Custis? Are you in there?"

Chapter 14

Longarm froze with the whip lifted above his head. On the bed beside him, Lady Margaret looked back over her shoulder with a heavy-lidded smile and said, "Why don't you invite her to join us, Custis? She's quite lovely, you know, and three people can do things that two can only dream of."

"Custis?" Emmaline repeated from the hallway. The doorknob rattled.

"Damn!" Longarm exploded. In his surprise at seeing Lady Margaret in his bed, he had closed the door behind him but had failed to wedge a chair under the knob. And he had forgotten for the moment that the door had no lock. . . .

It swung open as Longarm started to turn around.

Emmaline stood there, wrapped in the same silken robe Longarm had seen her wear before, the top half of it gaping open tantalizingly. He could only imagine what the scene must look like to her: him standing naked next to the bed, his manhood jutting out stiffly from his groin and a whip in his hand, while Lady Margaret, equally nude, wiggled around with her rump stuck up in the air.

"Emmaline, it ain't what it looks like," Longarm blurted

142

out, then immediately felt foolish. He added sheepishly, "Well, yeah, I reckon it probably is, but—"

"That's quite all right, Custis," Emmaline cut in coldly. "You're just indulging your desires so that impurities don't build up in your body. Isn't that what Sir Alfred would call it?"

Longarm tossed the whip aside. "I don't care what Sir Alfred calls it," he said. "I never meant to hurt you, Emmaline."

"Hurt me instead, Custis," Lady Margaret practically moaned.

Longarm turned toward her, grabbed the sheet, and yanked it up so that at least some of her body was covered. "Hush up," he snapped.

"Custis!" she exclaimed, clearly offended by his tone and his refusal to go through with what she wanted.

When Longarm swung around toward the door, he saw that Emmaline was already going back across the hall to her room. He bit back a curse and leaned over to snatch his trousers off the floor where Lady Margaret had dropped them earlier. Hurriedly, he pulled them on, hopping toward the hallway as he did so.

"Emmaline," he called after her. "Hang on a minute."

She went into her room and slammed the door behind her.

Longarm pulled up his trousers, buttoned them, and said, "Son of a bitch."

"Yes," Lady Margaret said icily from the bed, "you appear to be."

Without looking at her, Longarm said, "Why don't you get dressed, Your Ladyship? I don't reckon there's going to be any cavorting going on around here tonight."

"I should say not," she sniffed.

Longarm left her there and strode across the corridor. He balled his right hand into a fist and rapped his knuckles sharply on the door. "Emmaline," he said, "I want to talk to you."

He figured she would ignore him, at least for a few minutes, but the door was jerked open almost immediately. Her robe was pulled closed all up and down, he noticed, and the belt around her waist was tied tighter than it had been a few moments earlier. "What do you want?" she asked.

"To tell you again that I didn't mean to cause you any hurt," said Longarm. "I ain't in the habit of apologizing for the gals I bed down with, and I don't figure to start now. But . . . I wish I'd done things a mite different tonight."

Emmaline looked at him intently for a couple of seconds; then she sighed. "I don't suppose I have any right to be angry," she said. "You and I certainly don't have any claim on each other. I just thought that since we had enjoyed ourselves so much . . ."

"We surely did," Longarm agreed.

"Perhaps I read more into that than was really there." She managed a weak smile. "At any rate, Custis, I don't think that tonight will be a night of passion for us after all."

Longarm sighed heavily. "You're sure?"

"I'm certain."

"That's a pure-dee shame, but I reckon I understand." Longarm started to back off from the door. "Good night, Emmaline."

"Good night, Custis." She closed the door softly.

Someone bumped into Longarm from behind. "Yes, Custis," said Lady Margaret, her words as chilly as the runoff in a mountain stream when the snow starts to melt in the spring. "Good night. Sleep well . . . alone."

She had pulled on a nearly transparent robe, which he supposed was all she had worn to his room. She stalked away now, and as he watched her go, he had to admit that the view was pretty enticing. If anything, the fact that she was mad as a hornet made her backside twitch even more.

"Better not even think about that, old son," he advised himself. With a solemn shake of his head, he went back in his room and closed the door.

144

Since he wasn't going to be doing anything more plea-surable tonight, Longarm lit a cheroot, blew out the lamp, and sat down in one of the chairs to think about the theory he had worked out over the past couple of days. He didn't have all the answers to his questions, but enough of them so that a picture had definitely begun to emerge. As far as he could see, all the major loose ends were knitted up good and proper. The numbers he had found in the book in Sir Alfred's study had been the clincher.

Even before that, he had been convinced enough he was right so that he had gone ahead and put his plan into mo-tion. Arresting Obadiah Jones and having Sheriff Banning throw him in jail had been only the first step. Now it was a matter of having a little patience.

And doing a little more snooping. . . .

Lady Margaret was still mad at him the next morning when he went down to breakfast. She glared at him from the other end of the table. Longarm pretty much ignored her, though. She could always turn to Mark Hanley for consolation.

Longarm was more concerned with Emmaline, and he was glad to see that she greeted him with a smile. "Good morning," she said as he sat down next to her.

"Mornin'," Longarm replied. He wasn't sure yet how good it was going to be, but he had hopes.

"You're going back to Denver today, aren't you?" There was a hint of regret in her voice as she asked the question.

"Got to," he said.

"And I don't suppose you'll be coming this way again any time soon?"

"I'm sure when I get back to the office my boss'll have some other chore he needs me to attend to. Billy never has been one to let moss grow under the feet of his deputies." Longarm glanced down at the plate a servant put in front of him. "Which is probably a good thing, or else Sir Alfred would have us eating it," he added in a near-whisper.

That brought a laugh from Emmaline, and Longarm enjoyed the sound. He was going to miss her.

He just hoped that when she found out he had tricked her, she wouldn't be too angry.

Sir Alfred came in shortly, along with several more guests. The table was full now. Everyone made small talk until the meal was just about over; then Sir Alfred picked up his spoon and clinked it against the cup of evil-tasting green liquid that accompanied nearly every meal. The clear, ringing sound got the attention of everyone at the table. Sir Alfred stood up and began to speak.

"As you no doubt all are aware by now, the gentleman you all thought of as Mr. Custis Parker is in actuality none other than United States Deputy Marshal Custis Long. I apologize for deceiving you as to the true identity of a fellow guest here at Briarcliff Manor, but I can tell you now that *I* was the one who requested that a federal lawman be sent here and that he conduct an investigation into a matter that has been most troubling to me." Sir Alfred paused dramatically, then said, "Unknown to any of you here, my life has been in danger for the past several weeks."

That brought a murmur from the assembled guests, but nothing like the surprised reaction Sir Alfred seemed to have been expecting. The gossiping that had been going on since Longarm had revealed his identity the previous afternoon had made just about everyone aware of the trouble that had brought him to Briarcliff Manor.

Sir Alfred went on. "Now, thanks to Marshal Long, I can breathe much easier. The man who sought my death has been identified and taken into custody. And so . . ." He reached down and picked up his cup. "I say, here's to Marshal Long, with congratulations for a job well done!"

The guests raised their cups and echoed, "Here's to Marshal Long!" Even Lady Margaret, though she still wore a sullen expression on her face.

Longarm nodded his thanks as they all drank to him, but he left his own cup untouched on the table. "I'm much obliged for the sentiment," he said. He felt a little guilty, being toasted like that when he hadn't even finished the job yet, but he couldn't say anything about that without putting his plan in danger. All he could do was smile and nod and feel like a big fraud.

One of the guests, the female half of the elderly couple who had been carrying on like they were forty years younger, leaned forward and said eagerly, "Tell us how you caught the miscreant, Marshal."

"I reckon I just sort of plugged away until I figured things out," said Longarm, growing more uncomfortable. "That's pretty much the way most lawmen work."

"I heard that your own life was in danger," one of the men said. "Tell us about that."

"Not much to tell. The fella tried to bushwhack me, but I'm still here."

Sir Alfred laughed. "Now, now, no false modesty, Marshal. I imagine it was a rather thrilling adventure."

Suddenly, Longarm felt a flash of anger. "It sure as hell wasn't anything like what you read about in the dime novels," he said. "Until a bullet goes right by your head, you don't know what it's like. You just do what your instincts and your training tell you to do, and it ain't until later, when you stop and think about how close you came to dying, that your knees get a little weak and you notice that your hand shakes a mite when you go to pick something up. It goes away in a while if you're lucky. If it don't, you might as well turn in your badge, because you'll never be fit for this line of work. Some men ain't, and that's nothing against 'em. Could be the ones who stay in it are just too stubborn—or too dumb—to do anything else."

There was silence around the table as he finished talking. He'd never been the speechifying sort, and he wished now that he'd just kept his mouth shut and not let his irritation out. But it was too late for that. What was done was done.

After a moment, Sir Alfred cleared his throat. "Well said,

Marshal," he declared. "And now, I think it would be best if we end this discussion."

Longarm nodded, grateful for that decision.

"After all, you have a train to catch this morning. I took the liberty of checking the schedule for you, and the north-bound arrives in Trinidad at 11:07 and departs for Denver at approximately 11:14."

"I'll be on it with Jones," Longarm said. That, at least, was one promise he intended to keep.

It didn't take him long to pack once the meal was over. He threw everything into his war bag and came back down-stairs. Sir Alfred had asked him to step into the study before he left, so that was where Longarm went.

"Come in," the Englishman called in response to Long-arm's knock. He was seated behind his desk, but he stood up as Longarm entered the room.

"I reckon I'm just about ready to leave," said Longarm.

"I thought about offering you an honorarium for your services to me," said Sir Alfred, "but I was afraid that I would only offend you."

"If you're talking about paying me extra, I can't go along with that," Longarm replied with a shake of his head. "I collect my pay from Uncle Sam, and that's enough."

Sir Alfred smiled. "Just as I thought. An honorable man to the end." He stuck out his hand. "Farewell, Marshal Long. Know that you are always welcome here at Briarcliff Manor, should you ever wish to return."

"Much obliged." Longarm shook hands with him and left the study.

He hadn't seen Emmaline since breakfast, and he didn't want to leave without saying good-bye to her. Maybe that was what *she* wanted, though. Considering the incident the night before with Lady Margaret, Emmaline might have decided that it would be better not to be alone with him again.

However, as he stepped out the front door of the manor house, there she was, obviously waiting for him. The wagon was parked in the drive in front of the house, but Oscar was nowhere in sight. The former foreman of the ranch that Briarcliff Manor had once been must have wandered off to give Longarm a little privacy for his farewell with Emmaline. Longarm had to feel a touch of gratitude for that.

"Custis . . ." she said, stepping toward him and lifting a hand tentatively.

Longarm set the carpetbag on the ground at his feet. He reached out to take Emmaline's hand. "The best thing about this job," he said, "has been meeting you."

A smile curved her full red lips. "And you've been wonderful, Custis. In all my travels, all over the world, I don't believe I've ever met a man like you." She caught her breath suddenly, her eyes widening. "I . . . I just had an idea. Why don't you come back here after you deliver your prisoner to Denver, and then you can go on with me to San Francisco?"

Longarm shook his head regretfully. "Told you my boss will have something else for me to do when I get back."

"Then quit your job."

A frown creased his forehead. "Stop being a lawman? It's all I've done for a long time, Emmaline. I reckon I'm too set in my ways to take up a new line of work now."

"Nonsense," she said, a hint of desperation creeping into her voice. "You could be the supervisor of an archaeological dig anywhere in the world. We always need someone competent to run the expedition and see to the supplies and deal with the native workers and . . . and . . ." She sighed in resignation. "And that's not at all the sort of work you'd be happy doing, is it?"

"Like I said," Longarm told her as he cupped her chin in his hand, "I'm set in my ways." He leaned over and kissed her.

The kiss was long and deep and passionate, lacking perhaps in the urgency that would have preceded lovemaking, but still powerful enough to leave Longarm feeling it in his belly as he finally pulled away from her. "So long, Emmaline," he said.

She whispered, "Good-bye, Custis."

She turned then and went quickly into the house, and Oscar emerged a moment later. "Ready to go, Marshal?" he asked.

"Ready," replied Longarm. "And I appreciate the privacy."

Oscar winked at him. "Figured you'd have some good-byes to say," he said with a grin.

Longarm tossed his carpetbag onto the first of the bench seats, then asked Oscar, "Mind if I ride on the box with you?"

"Nope. I knew right off you weren't the usual sort of guest Sir Alfred gets up here."

Both men climbed onto the driver's seat, and Oscar took up the reins and got the team moving. Longarm didn't look back at Briarcliff Manor as they left it behind. Instead he watched the landscape on both sides of the road.

"I'll bet this was a pretty good spread when those Englishmen owned it and you were running the place," he commented.

Oscar shrugged. "We had a good herd built up. Shipped a lot of beef back East. But them days are over, I reckon."

"Things change," said Longarm.

"Yeah. They do."

When they reached Trinidad, Longarm stepped down from the seat, retrieved his bag, and then reached up to shake hands with Oscar. "Thanks for all your help," he said.

"So long, Marshal. Have a good trip back to Denver."

Longarm started to turn away, then glanced back and added, "Say so long to Jed for me, would you?"

"Sure thing," promised Oscar.

The wagon had stopped in front of the sheriff's office, so Longarm went inside and found Sheriff Banning pouring a cup of coffee. He didn't offer a cup to Longarm. Instead he just grunted and asked, "You come to pick up Obadiah?"

"That's right," Longarm said.

"I still think you're making a mistake."

"Jones had a motive, he's got the right kind of rifle, and he was nowhere around when somebody was trying to kill me. I'd say that's plenty of evidence."

"I asked him where he was that afternoon," Banning said. "He claims he'd gone up into the hills to pray."

"To p-r-e-y, is more like it," said Longarm.

Banning grimaced. "I see I ain't going to change your mind. All right, Marshal. Do what you've got to do. But I sure don't agree with it."

"Nobody's asking you to."

The air in the sheriff's office was decidedly cool and unfriendly as Banning unlocked the cell block door and then brought Obadiah Jones out of his cell. The preacher was unshaven and looked even gaunter and more wild-eyed than usual. "Come to cast me into the lion's den?" he said bitterly to Longarm.

"Come on," Longarm said curtly. He didn't feel like arguing with the man.

Jones was handcuffed. Longarm gripped his arm tightly and led him out of the jail. He was aware of the stares from some of the townspeople as he marched the reverend down the street to the train station. Longarm heard the whistle of the locomotive as the northbound pulled in. He was glad that he wouldn't have to spend much more time in Trinidad.

Within ten minutes, the train was rolling north, taking with it two new passengers.

An hour later, the northbound stopped in Walsenburg, the first good-sized settlement after Trinidad and the county seat of Huerfano County. That meant there was a sheriff's office here too, since Arch Banning was the sheriff of Las Animas County. Longarm was counting on the cooperation of the local lawman as he got to his feet and pulled Jones upright.

"Come on," he said. "We're going to the sheriff's office."

"This isn't Denver," Jones protested.

"I know that. We ain't going to Denver."

"But . . . but you said—"

"I say a lot of things. Now let's go."

Longarm took the preacher off the train and asked one of the porters where he could find the sheriff's office. The man directed him down the street. Walsenburg wasn't as big as Trinidad, so Longarm had no trouble finding the place he was looking for.

The Huerfano County sheriff was a heavyset man in late middle age with white hair and a sweeping walrus mustache. "You want me to do what?" he asked in surprise after Longarm had identified himself and requested help.

"Just hold this fella here in your jail until tomorrow," Longarm said again. "Then let him go, rent a horse for him, and send the bill to the chief Marshal's office in Denver."

"I never heard of such," said the star packer. "Why arrest a feller and then let him go again?"

"I got my reasons," Longarm said. His tone of voice made it clear that he didn't intend to explain them either.

The sheriff blew out a sigh, fluttering his mustache. "Well, if this don't beat all. I reckon I'll do it, seein' as how you're a federal man and all, but damned if I understand it."

"Thanks, Sheriff. If I get a chance, I'll stop back by here and explain it all to you later."

Jones lifted both handcuffed hands and pointed at Longarm. "This man does the work of Satan!" he declared.

"No, but I'll agree with you on one thing, preacher," Longarm said. "Sometimes you can't tell by looking who's a devil and who ain't."

With that bit of wisdom dispensed, Longarm left the office and headed for the livery stable across the street. It took him only a few minutes to rent a big chestnut gelding, along with a saddle and tack, and as soon as he swung up onto the horse's back, he heeled it into a trot, riding quickly out of Walsenburg and heading south again, toward Trinidad.

And Briarcliff Manor.

Chapter 15

Longarm's path paralleled the railroad tracks most of the way. It took twice as long to cover the distance between Walsenburg and Trinidad on horseback as it had by rail, so it was nearing mid-afternoon when Longarm swung off the main trail north of Trinidad and headed up into the foot-hills. From there he would make his own way. He didn't think anyone would be watching for his return, but a fella could never tell. It was better to be careful, especially when there were .50-caliber slugs involved.

He steered his course by a distant mountain he knew to be Culebra Peak. The peak was due west of Briarcliff Manor, and that was the direction from which Longarm wanted to approach the health retreat. He circled, zigzagged back and forth, and generally made his way the best he could through the rugged terrain. As he reckoned he was drawing closer to Briarcliff Manor, he grew more alert, fig-uring that he would find what he was looking for some-where in this area.

Broad, grassy valleys stretched between the foothills. This was prime ranching country, thought Longarm. It was a damned shame it was just sitting here empty.

Likely somebody else had thought the same thing—and done something about it.

He was certain now he was on range that was part of the ranch that had become Briarcliff Manor. He rode from one valley to the next, checking out each of them as he came to them. However, despite his watchfulness, he almost missed the narrow, sharply angled slash through a rocky ridge that led into one of the most idyllic settings he had run across in a long time. The path through the ridge was barely a dozen feet wide, with sheer rocky walls on both sides that rose more than a hundred feet. The sky overhead was just a tiny blue line. The trail twisted torturously over its quarter-mile length, but when it ended, another of the broad valleys opened before Longarm's eyes, the entrance into it barred by a wooden gate.

This was a box canyon, walled by cliffs on both sides and at the far end. At that far end, a stream tumbled over the brink in a towering waterfall that sparkled brilliantly in the afternoon sun. At the base of the waterfall was a small natural lake, and from it flowed a stream that watered the rest of the valley and caused the grass here to grow thick and lush and green. There was one other thing Longarm noticed immediately about the valley.

It was full of cattle.

Everywhere Longarm looked, he saw clumps of fine-looking stock grazing on the grass. Without even attempting to count them, he could make an estimate of their number: 3800. Too many even for a valley such as this one; in time they would over-graze it. But for a few months, they could survive easily in these gorgeous surroundings.

Longarm sat on the rented horse and rested his left hand on the horn while he used his right to push back his Stetson. He was completely convinced now that his theory was right. Here was yet more evidence, not just mere numbers this time but living, breathing proof-on-the-hoof.

He leaned down from the saddle, unlatched the gate, and swung it open enough for him to ride through and enter the valley. He closed it behind him, not wanting any of the cows to stray into the confining passage through which he had come. It couldn't have been easy, driving the cattle through that ugly slash in the ridge, and probably short-handed at that. But the men he was after had done it.

Longarm's keen eyes scanned the valley. He caught sight of a thin plume of smoke off to the left. He rode in that direction, and after a few minutes he spotted some sort of building through a stand of trees. He dismounted and went closer, leading the horse now.

A faint whiff of woodsmoke came to him, carrying with it the smell of something else. Longarm sniffed. It took him only a second to recognize the distinctive smell of hair being singed. He had experienced it enough during his days as a cowboy that he would never forget it. That smoke was from a branding fire.

The chestnut began to get a little skittish. Longarm calmed the horse as best he could, and left it tied to a sapling. Better to go on without it than risk the horse giving away his presence with a loud whinny at the wrong time. The chestnut was cropping contentedly on the grass when Longarm slipped away into the trees.

He catfooted toward the building he had spotted, and then crouched behind some brush, parting the branches to get a better look. About fifty yards away stood a log cabin with a good-sized corral and shed behind it. The cabin had a chimney, but no smoke was coming from it. The smoke Longarm had seen earlier was rising from someplace beyond the cabin.

Several horses were in the corral. Longarm's eyes narrowed as he studied them. One of them, he saw, was a chestnut with a white blaze on its face. It would have been interesting to take a look at the horse's brand. Longarm would have been willing to bet that it belonged to the Wilcox Livery in Trinidad. He was certain he was looking at the mount that had been rented by Dr. Ulrich Ganz for his fatal ride back out to Briarcliff Manor.

Longarm heard men's voices in the distance. The cabin seemed to be deserted, so he risked leaving the cover of the trees and ran toward the structure, crouching over slightly as he did so. He made it to the cabin and put his back against the log wall, reaching across his body to slide the Colt .45 from the cross-draw rig as he did so.

Cautiously, Longarm slid along the wall toward the front of the cabin. When he got to the corner of the building, he took his hat off and edged his head out for a quick look-see. A hundred yards away was another corral, this one with cattle in it. A small branding fire burned near the corral. Longarm saw two men on horseback and two men on foot, but he didn't recognize any of them. One of the riders roped a steer in the corral and led him out through a gate opened by one of the men on foot. The other man on the ground took a running iron from the fire. As Longarm watched, the steer's feet were roped and it was jerked over on its side and held still by the two horsebackers. The man with the running iron approached it and worked quickly, searing the steer's flank with the red-hot metal. The animal let out a bawl of pain.

The whole setup was damned clever, thought Longarm, and it was just as he had expected it to be. These men were blotting the brands on the cattle, changing each original brand into a different one. In the hands of a talented rustler, a running iron could alter a brand so that practically no one would ever be aware of the change just by looking at the animal in question. The inside of the hide told a different story, but the cow had to be dead and skinned before that ever came to light.

And there wouldn't be any reason for anyone to be suspicious about where these cattle came from either. When they showed up again, everything would seem to be open and aboveboard.

Longarm smiled grimly. Give the fellas credit, he thought. They had come up with a pretty good scheme, and it was just too bad that some folks had to die in order for it to work.

A rock rattled quietly behind Longarm.

That was enough of a warning to make him start to spin around. From the corner of his eye, he saw a figure lunging toward him, saw a piece of firewood descending toward his head. Longarm threw his right arm up in a desperate attempt to block the blow. The firewood cracked against his wrist and his hand went numb. The Colt slipped from his fingers. He stumbled back against the wall.

Jed slashed at him again with the firewood. The old man's mouth was pulled back in a toothless grimace. Longarm ducked under the blow. Jed chopped at him, and this time the firewood scraped the side of Longarm's head.

"Steve! Brinker!" screamed the old man in his high, wavering voice. "Dunaway! Garcia! Damn it, get over here!"

Longarm figured those were the four men working at the branding fire. If they heard Jed's shouts—and Longarm didn't see how they could fail to hear—they would come running to see what was wrong. The two men on horseback could get there in a hurry too. So there was no time to waste.

Longarm's foot lashed out in a kick aimed at Jed's groin. Jed twisted with surprising agility for a man of his age and took the blow on his thigh. It was still enough to knock him backward, off his feet. He screamed for help again as he sprawled on his back. Longarm started past him at a run, heading for the corral behind the cabin. He didn't have time to retrieve the chestnut he had tied in the trees, so he would have to take one of the horses from the corral if he wanted a chance to get out of there.

As he went past Jed, though, the old man latched on to Longarm's right ankle. Jed yanked on it as hard as he could, spilling Longarm off his feet. The big lawman landed heavily, knocking the wind out of him. He tried to jerk his leg away from Jed, but the old man was hanging on like a leech and bellowing for help all the time.

A horse pounded around the corner of the cabin. The man in the saddle had a gun in his hand. He yelled, "What the hell!" at the sight of Jed struggling with a stranger on the ground.

"Help me!" Jed screeched.

Longarm finally succeeded in freeing his foot from Jed's claw-like grip. He spotted the revolver he had dropped on the ground and rolled toward it, reaching out with his left hand for the weapon. Suddenly the horse loomed over him, and Longarm was forced to abandon his attempt for the Colt and roll against the wall of the cabin to escape the slashing, iron-shod hooves of the animal.

"Don't kill him! You hear me? Don't kill him!"

That was Jed again, hollering orders. A few moments earlier, when he had been trying to bash Longarm's skull in with that length of firewood, he hadn't seemed to be so worried about killing the lawman. Now he was insistent, however.

The other rider had arrived, and both men on horseback leveled their six-guns at Longarm. He had no choice but to pull himself into a sitting position against the wall and lift his hands in surrender. It was galling, but they had the drop on him. The other two men came running up. One of them, a stout Mexican in a sombrero and a *charro* jacket, held a Winchester that he had grabbed up from somewhere. The other one was brandishing an old Dragoon Colt. They joined the two horsebackers in covering Longarm with their guns.

"One o' you boys give me a hand, doggone it," complained Jed. "I ain't as young as I used to be."

"You ain't been young since Methuselah was a pup," one of the men said with a grin. He jabbed the barrel of his pistol toward Longarm. "Who's this here *buscadero*?"

The Mexican helped Jed to his feet, and the old hostler glared down at Longarm. "A young feller who's too damn nosy for his own good." To Longarm, he said, "I thought you went back to Denver."

"I reckon that's what I wanted you to think," Longarm said dryly. He flexed the fingers of his right hand. The feeling was coming back onto them now, and as he rotated his wrist he could tell that nothing was broken. The hand worked fine. He just wished he could wrap it around the butt of a gun right about now.

"What in blazes do we do with him?" asked one of the riders.

"He's seen what we're doing up here," said the other horsebacker. "I say we kill him."

"Not yet," snapped Jed. "Tie him up and put him in the cabin. I'll keep an eye on him until Oscar gets here in a little while." He leaned over and spat. "We'll let *him* decide what to do with the son of a bitch."

They trussed Longarm up like one of those cattle ready for branding and hauled him into the cabin. It was a typical cow-country line shack with four narrow bunks, a stove, a table, a couple of rough-hewn chairs, and a few shelves on the wall that held supplies. Steve, Brinker, Dunaway, and Garcia could live here, but not particularly comfortably. Longarm wondered if they got a break occasionally and rode up to Walsenburg or Pueblo for some carousing. That was likely.

Nobody was in any mood for celebrating now, however. The men were grim-faced as they tossed Longarm onto the dirt floor of the shack and left him there. Jed picked up a double-barreled shotgun from the table and tucked it under his arm, turning so that the twin barrels of the Greener were pointed in Longarm's general direction.

"I'll keep an eye on him," Jed declared. "He ain't goin' nowhere."

"Better make it a close eye, old-timer," advised one of the men.

"Dag nab it, I'm the one who spotted him slinkin' around here and got the drop on him, ain't I, Steve?" Jed said indignantly. "Don't you go makin' out like I'm useless. When it looked like you boys was goin' to have to go back to bein' poor ol' grub-line riders, it was me an' Oscar who came up with the plan, weren't it?"

"Yeah," said the Mexican, who had only a faint accent, "but you couldn't've pulled it off without us, *viejo*."

Jed bristled again, but the other four men filed out of the shack without paying any attention to him. When they had gone back to their brand-blotting, Jed turned to Longarm and said, "Bunch of ungrateful pups."

"Folks just don't appreciate a good rustling operation anymore, do they?" Longarm asked as he squirmed himself into a sitting position.

Jed frowned. "We ain't rustlin' nothin'. Them cows is ours by right."

"What right?" asked Longarm. "They belonged to that English syndicate first of all, and then to Sir Alfred."

"That feller!" Jed waved his free hand dismissively. "He's crazy, I tell you, crazy as a loon. You've seen the food he makes folks eat. And all that carryin'-on, like the Rockin' H was nothin' but a fancy whorehouse."

"The Rocking H? That was the brand before Brundage bought the ranch?"

"Yep. Oscar an' me an' those boys you saw outside worked our asses off for years to make it one o' the best spreads in Colorado, an' then what happens? That damned syndicate sells it right out from under us!" Jed started to pace back and forth angrily. "But we weren't goin' to stand for that, nosirreebob!"

"When Sir Alfred told Oscar to sell off the stock, Oscar only sold half of it, right?" Longarm said. "Then he and those other punchers moved the rest of it up here to this valley?" As long as he was stuck in the cabin with the talkative old man, he might as well take advantage of the situation to confirm some of his guesses, Longarm figured.

"That's right," Jed replied proudly. "And that damn-fool Englishman didn't have a clue we'd done it neither. He never even checked the tally book."

"I did," said Longarm. "Oscar shouldn't have left it in

161

Sir Alfred's study. Sir Alfred might not know what the numbers in it mean, but a fella who's ever done any cowboying would recognize 'em at first glance."

Jed frowned. "How'd you know how many head we sold?"

Longarm had planned to ask the questions, not answer them, but he didn't see how it could do any harm to tell Jed the truth. "I wired my boss in Denver and had him check the records of sales at the Livestock Exchange. They showed that Oscar only sold a little more than half of the cattle that were listed in the tally book."

"How'd you know he sold 'em through the Exchange?"

"Didn't, for sure," admitted Longarm. "But the difference in the numbers was enough to make me want to take a look around and see if I could find the rest of the herd, if it was still here." He leaned his head toward the outside of the cabin. "Sure enough, it was."

"I thought you was convinced that preacher feller was behind all the trouble."

"That's what I wanted you to think. And for a while, I really did believe Jones was the one who'd bushwhacked me and tried to kill Sir Alfred. But I've been around long enough to know that most of the time more folks kill for money than they do because something offends their religious beliefs."

"What about that there Inquisition over yonder in Spain?"

Longarm was a little surprised that Jed had even heard of the Inquisition, but he shrugged and replied, "I said most of the time. Not always."

Hoofbeats sounded outside. Two horses, Longarm judged. They came to a stop, and a moment later the door of the cabin was jerked open. "I found a horse tied in the woods," Oscar said as he stalked into the room. "What in hell—" He stopped short as he caught sight of Longarm sitting on the floor, tied hand and foot and propped up against the wall. "What's he doin' here?"

"He's figgered it all out, Oscar," Jed said. "I still ain't quite sure how he done it, but he knows what we been doin'."

Oscar frowned darkly at Longarm. "Is that true, Marshal?"

It wouldn't do any good to lie now. Longarm said coolly, "I reckon I know most of it."

"He done told me he checked the tally book and saw we'd kept back half the herd," Jed put in. "That's why he come lookin' for 'em."

Longarm said, "I know about how you've been trying to kill Sir Alfred too, and how you murdered Ganz. I saw the horse he rented in that shed out back."

"Damn it!" Oscar bit out. "I knew we should've got rid of that horse." He sighed and thumbed back his battered old Stetson. "I was goin' to take it back closer to town and turn it loose. It would've found its way back to Wilcox's. Just hadn't got around to it yet."

"What I ain't quite sure of," said Longarm, "is why Sir Alfred had to die. You could've made a pretty penny changing those brands and selling off what was left of the herd a little at a time."

"It's not enough," snapped Oscar. "That's what we had in mind at first, but after Brundage nearly stumbled over this valley and we had to start that rock slide to scare him off, I got to figuring what would happen if he'd accidentally wound up dead."

"You and your pards could take over the ranch again, maybe run it for whoever inherited from Sir Alfred, or maybe even buy it outright with the money you could get from selling off some more of the herd," speculated Longarm.

Oscar shrugged. "Seems to us that we got more of a right to the place than anybody else does."

"You tried again to get rid of Sir Alfred by setting up an accident with a runaway horse, but when that didn't work, you got impatient," Longarm went on. "You took a shot at him with an old buffalo gun."

"My brother was a buffalo hunter, back in Kansas," Oscar said. "I got his gun when he died of a fever a while back."

Longarm put the rest of it together with no trouble. "So when Reverend Jones started raising a ruckus about Briarcliff Manor, you figured you'd use that Sharps to kill Sir Alfred and the reverend would get the blame."

"Ain't that just what happened?" Oscar demanded. "You arrested him yourself and hauled him off to Denver."

"I'd figured out by then that he probably wasn't guilty, though. I was just trying to catch you off guard."

"And he would've too, if it wasn't for me!" Jed exclaimed. He cackled with laughter and shook the Greener's barrels at Longarm. "I caught you, didn't I, Marshal?"

"You surely did," Longarm admitted.

Oscar took off his hat and ran his fingers through his gray hair as he frowned in thought. "What the hell are we goin' to do with you?" he asked.

Longarm knew not to waste his breath suggesting that they let him go. He had uncovered their plan, and the only way they could be safe in the future was if he was no longer around to threaten them.

"I say we kill him," Jed said.

"Then why didn't you take care of that before I got here?" Oscar wanted to know.

Jed rubbed his grizzled jaw. "Well, now, I thought about it. But then I figgered you might have some other use for him. I ain't as smart as you, Oscar. I've always knowed that."

Oscar hunkered down on his heels in front of Longarm. "It's a damned shame you had to come back here, Marshal," he said. "I didn't mind so much killin' that son of a bitch Ganz. A fella that nasty sort of needs killin' most of the time. But like I told you earlier today, I could tell right from the first that you weren't like all those other folks at Briarcliff Manor."

"That didn't stop you from trying to bushwhack me when I was on my way back from Trinidad," Longarm pointed out.

Oscar grunted. "Well, I wasn't thinkin' too straight at first. All I knew was that you were pokin' around in things that didn't concern you. I'll admit that I was tryin' to plug you with that first shot. But then, after it missed, I got to thinkin' that maybe it'd be better if you *didn't* die just yet. So I started aimin' wide and high most of the time."

"Because you knew I'd recognize the sound of a buffalo gun and be more convinced than ever that Jones was the bushwhacker," Longarm guessed. Well, that was one more question answered, he told himself.

"Yep," agreed Oscar. "I didn't know then that you were a lawman, but I knew if you were bound and determined to nose around, I wanted you sniffin' after Jones and not anybody else. Turned out you were even more clever than I thought, though."

"Not clever enough, I reckon," Longarm said wryly.

"Nope." Oscar straightened and pulled his Colt from its holster. As he eared back the hammer, he said, "Not near clever enough to keep from dyin'."

Chapter 16

Longarm's backbone felt like a rope made of ice as he saw the barrel of Oscar's pistol swing toward him. He'd been in plenty of tight spots before, situations that looked hopeless. This one was simple enough: a man with a gun in a log cabin. But it looked like it was going to finally mean Longarm's end.

Oscar hesitated, then burst out, "Aw, hell!" He lowered the gun. "I can't do it."

"Can't do it!" Jed burst out. "You didn't have no trouble sticking that carvin' knife in the back o' that Ganz fella when he overheard what we was sayin' in the stable."

"That was different," Oscar grated. "Like I said, Ganz was a son of a bitch, and stupid to boot. If he'd just slipped away instead of tryin' to gloat about what he'd found out, I'd've never had the chance to stick that knife in him."

Even with his insides cold and his nerves drawn taut, Longarm was glad to hear that one of his other guesses had been correct. Ganz had come back to Briarcliff Manor to try to steal that prehistoric skull from Emmaline, more than likely, but instead he had stumbled over the plan hatched by Oscar and Jed and died on account of it.

Longarm felt a small touch of queasiness as he realized the carving knife he had used to cut up that chunk of roast

Mrs. Hastings had given him had been used earlier that same evening to murder Ulrich Ganz. No wonder Oscar and Jed had lost their appetites and hadn't finished off the food after dumping Ganz in the mineral bath.

"Ganz is another fella who left and shouldn't have come back," Oscar went on. He lowered the hammer on his Colt and jammed the gun back in its holster. "I'm goin' back to the house. Jed, you and the rest of the boys take care of the marshal here."

"And just what are you goin' to be doin'?" Jed asked.

Oscar rubbed the back of his hand across his mouth. "I'll take care of Brundage. I'll have to go back to makin' it look like an accident, though, since we don't have Jones around to blame for it anymore. Shouldn't be too hard," he mused. "Brundage's guard'll be down. He thinks he's safe again, what with the preacher on his way to jail."

Longarm bit back a groan. Oscar was right. It would be easier than ever now to murder Sir Alfred, and that was partially Longarm's fault. If he hadn't let that stove-up old hostler get the drop on him . . .

"Come on back to the house when you're done here," Oscar told Jed. "We can't both be gone too long."

Jed nodded. "Don't you worry none, Oscar. I'll take care of things good an' proper." He hefted the Greener.

Longarm suppressed a shudder. He had seen what one of those weapons could do to a man at close range. Both barrels would pretty much blow him in half or take his head right off his shoulders, whichever way Jed decided to go.

Oscar stalked out, and a minute later Longarm heard hoofbeats again as he rode away. Jed came over to him and chuckled. "That Oscar's got him a soft heart," he said. "That's his problem. He's smart as a whip, but he ain't got enough of a killin' streak in him."

"He's planning to murder Sir Alfred tonight, and he killed Ganz," Longarm pointed out.

"That Englisher's got to be got rid of, and the business with Ganz happened sort of on the spur o' the moment, I reckon you could say. Oscar didn't have no time to think about what he was doin'. But if he hadn't killed Ganz, I would've." Jed grinned. "I don't mind killin' folks when I have to. But I'll be damned if I'm goin' to splatter blood and brains all over this cabin, because I know who the boys'd make clean it all up, yessirree. We'll just drag you outside 'fore we blow your head clean off."

Jed turned toward the door, obviously intending to summon the other men to help him. He was still too close to Longarm, though. Longarm's legs, bound together at the ankles, snapped up and bent at the knees, then shot forward. The heels of his boots hit the backs of Jed's knees and knocked the old man's legs out from under him. Jed cried out in pain and surprise and pitched forward, dropping the Greener as he fell. The shotgun didn't go off when it landed on the dirt floor of the cabin, and Longarm was grateful for that. A shot would have brought the other men on the run.

He levered himself forward in an awkward dive and landed on top of Jed, who had fallen face-down. Longarm's knees drove into the small of Jed's back, pinning him to the ground. Jed lifted his head to scream for help, but before a sound could emerge from his mouth, Longarm looped his roped-together wrists over the old man's head and under his chin. He jerked up as hard as he could.

Jed's neck snapped with a crisp sound, like a dead branch breaking.

He went limp underneath Longarm, his fingers scrabbling in the dust for a couple of seconds before going still. Longarm pulled his arms back over Jed's head and then rolled to the side so that he could see the dull sheen of death in the old man's eyes. He didn't waste any time feeling sorry for Jed, remembering how gleeful the man had sounded when he mentioned blowing Longarm's head off.

Jed's one outcry had evidently gone unheard amidst the bawling of cattle having their brands altered. Still, there was always the chance that one of the cowboys could show up at any moment. Longarm crawled quickly over to the table and used it to steady himself as he climbed to his feet. He looked around and spotted a knife lying on the shelf with the supplies. He hopped over to it and picked it up, fumbling a little because of his bound wrists, then turned the blade and started sawing on the ropes.

The knife was fairly dull, but Longarm managed to cut through his bonds in about five minutes. That time seemed longer than it was. When his hands were finally free, he bent over and cut the ropes around his ankles. He hadn't been tied up long enough for any of his extremities to go numb, and he was thankful for that. His Colt was on the table. He picked it up and slipped it back into its holster.

He was free and one of his former captors was dead. But he was still a long way from being out of this mess, he knew. There were still four men out there, four armed and hardened range riders who had stepped over the line and become outlaws.

The cabin didn't have a back door, but it had a window. Longarm figured that was how Jed had managed to get behind him. Jed must have been in the cabin when Longarm approached. He had seen the big lawman, climbed out through the window, and gotten the drop on Longarm. Now Longarm picked up the shotgun and went to the window. He pushed the shutters open a little and peered out cautiously.

The window was on the opposite side of the cabin from the branding fire. That was a lucky break, one that Longarm intended to use to his advantage. He threw a long leg over the sill and stepped out, then moved carefully along the wall toward the corral. If he could get one of the horses and lead it into the woods before the others discovered he was gone . . .

"Jed! Damn it, what—"

The startled exclamation from inside made Longarm stop short and whirl back to the window. As he thrust the barrels of the Greener into the cabin, he saw one of the cowboys, the one called Steve, standing just inside the door, staring at Jed's sprawled body. Steve spotted Longarm at the window and clawed for the gun on his hip.

Longarm waited until the man's Colt had cleared leather before he touched one of the shotgun's triggers. The load of buckshot exploded from the weapon with a roar of black powder. Steve was thrown across the cabin and back through the open door by the blast, crimson flowers blooming abruptly across his chest and belly.

Well, that pretty much did away with the idea of stealth, thought Longarm. He spun around and ran toward the corral.

The gunfire had spooked the horses, making them dance around skittishly. Longarm threw the gate open, not caring if the others bolted as long as he was able to catch one of the animals. The saddle horse from Wilcox's Livery in Trinidad was probably the calmest of the bunch. Longarm stepped aside as a couple of the other horses thundered out of the corral, then moved into the enclosure and headed for the chestnut with the white blaze on its face.

The horse nervously tossed its head up and down, but it allowed Longarm to get fairly close before the Mexican came running around the cabin, six-gun blazing. Longarm went to a knee and fired the Greener's second barrel between the poles of the corral. The blast tore Garcia's legs out from under him and tumbled him to the ground in front of the open gate just as one of the other horses stampeded through it. Garcia threw up his arms and screamed, but the horse's iron-shod hooves crashed through that feeble barrier and thudded into his face, caving it in and leaving it only vaguely resembling something that had once been human. Garcia twitched a few times and died.

The chestnut was the only horse left in the corral. Longarm dropped the empty shotgun and grabbed its mane as it lunged past him. He held on tight and kicked with his feet, springing up and throwing a leg over the horse's back in as neat a running mount as anything a Pony Express rider had ever done. He leaned forward as something whipped past his ear, trying to make himself a smaller target. The other two men, Brinker and Dunaway, were firing at him.

Using his knees to steer and his left hand to hang on to the chestnut's mane as he rode bareback, Longarm drew his Colt and threw a couple of shots at Brinker and Dunaway, who dived behind a pile of firewood not far from the cabin door. Longarm caught a glimpse of Steve's bloody corpse lying half in and half out of the door, then turned the chestnut toward the trees. If he could manage to avoid the bullets Brinker and Dunaway were throwing at him, he stood an excellent chance of getting away. It would take them a few minutes to catch the horses that had bolted from the corral, and by that time Longarm would have a good lead on them. If they were smart, once they had taken a look around and seen the bodies of Jed, Steve, and Garcia, they would cut their losses and take off for the tall and uncut.

Longarm veered the horse into the pines. He cast a glimpse through the trees at the western sky. The sun was lowering toward the mountains now. In another hour it would be dark, and Oscar was on his way back to Briarcliff Manor to make another try at murdering Sir Alfred Brundage. He would probably wait until nightfall, thought Longarm, when all the guests would be occupied with other things. That would give Longarm at least a chance to get there in time.

Right now, after coming so close to death, a chance was all he wanted.

Sir Alfred Brundage retired to his study after dinner, as he did most evenings. Some of the guests had gone to the cleansing rooms, while others had already headed for their bedrooms on the second floor. Sir Alfred felt a moment of satisfaction as he thought about how they were no doubt purifying themselves by indulging their desires and thereby ridding themselves of them. As for himself, he had long

171

since freed himself from the demands of the flesh. He had led the life of a libertine for many years, and it had left him sated, quite content to surround himself with the pleasures of good books and the thinkers who had written them. He selected a volume of Shakespeare's sonnets, and sat down behind the desk to peruse the gorgeously flowing lines.

A knock sounded on the door of the study, and Oscar stuck his head into the room to say, "Uh, Boss, you reckon you could come with me for a spell?"

Sir Alfred looked up with a frown, marking his place in the book with a finger. He had barely gotten started reading, and he didn't much care for being interrupted. "What is it, Oscar?" he asked. "Can't it wait until morning?"

"Don't rightly see how. One of the guests is down at the mineral baths. He's slipped on the flagstones and hurt himself."

"Oh, dear Lord!" exclaimed Sir Alfred as he came to his feet. "Who is it?"

"Now, Boss, you know I don't recollect all the guests' names. It was that old fella—"

"Mr. Hargitty?"

"That's him, all right," Oscar said with a nod. "I was on my way to the stable when I heard him yell for help. When I went to see to him, I could tell right away his leg was broke. That's when I came here on the double to fetch you."

Sir Alfred dropped the book of sonnets on the desk, its appeal forgotten in this moment of crisis. "You did the correct thing," he said to Oscar as he hurried out from behind the desk. "Come along. We'll bring poor Mr. Hargitty back up here to the house and make him as comfortable as possible before we send someone to Trinidad for the doctor."

"You're a sawbones, ain't you?" said Oscar as they walked quickly along the corridor toward the rear of the house. "Couldn't you set his leg?"

"Well, yes, I suppose I could, but I haven't practiced that

172

sort of medicine in many years. I'll do what I can for him, but I'd prefer that a physician more familiar with such injuries do any setting of bones."

Oscar nodded. "Reckon that's a good idea." He opened the rear door and stepped back to let Sir Alfred go first. The Englishman bustled out into the darkness with Oscar trailing behind him.

That way, Sir Alfred didn't see the ruthless grin that briefly touched Oscar's face before he followed Sir Alfred into the night.

Emmaline Colton saw it, however, as she stepped out of the kitchen. She was already hungry despite the recent meal, and had come there to look for something more substantial to eat. She believed in Sir Alfred's methods, at least to a certain extent, but the diet at Briarcliff Manor sometimes left a person feeling unsatisfied.

Tonight, Emmaline felt unsatisfied in a different way. She missed Custis Long already, missed the solid, muscular warmth of his body, missed the feeling of his manhood thrusting into her and filling her until it reached her very core.

She knew that thoughts such as those would only make things worse, so she had gone to the kitchen, hoping to satisfy her other appetites and distract herself in the process. Mrs. Hastings had already finished cleaning up for the evening and had gone to her room, and Emmaline had been unable to find anything good to eat. Now, with a sigh, she left the kitchen—

And stopped short as she saw Sir Alfred and Oscar leaving the house through the rear door. Neither of the men seemed to have noticed her, so intent were they on something else. Oscar, especially, had a positively bloodthirsty look on his face, Emmaline thought. What in heaven's name could be wrong?

Distraction was what she was after, and distraction was what she seemed to have found. Without a word, she followed the two men, slipping out through the door that Oscar hadn't completely closed behind him.

A big prairie moon had risen in the east, casting a silvery glow over the garden. Still, even with that illumination, Emmaline could not see Sir Alfred and Oscar. She was able to follow them by the sounds of their footsteps on the gravel walk, however. She went after them, deciding in a moment that they were heading toward the mineral baths.

A shudder went through Emmaline as she remembered what had happened there two nights previously. The lovemaking with Custis had been sublime, but the memory of it would always be marred by the grisly discovery that had followed. Emmaline had wept a few tears, not for the man Ulrich Ganz had become, but for the man he had been in the past, when the two of them were together. Perhaps she had been blind to his real nature, but that didn't really matter. Her feelings for him had been genuine at the time.

Even though she didn't particularly want to return to the mineral baths, her curiosity compelled her to keep following Sir Alfred and Oscar. If there was more trouble, Emmaline wanted to know about it, and the two men had certainly been moving as if their mission was urgent. She heard their voices and came a little closer, realizing that they had stopped beside one of the pools.

"But I don't understand," Sir Alfred was saying. "Where is Mr. Hargitty?"

"I'm afraid he's not here, Doc." That was Oscar, and something about his voice in the darkness made Emmaline frown. He sounded different somehow, dangerous. His next words confirmed that. "Don't move now. I don't want to shoot you."

"My God!" exclaimed Sir Alfred. "What are you doing? Put down that gun this instant, Oscar."

Emmaline froze where she was, knowing she did not dare come any closer.

" 'Fraid I can't do that, Boss."

"What is this about?" Sir Alfred demanded. "You come

into the house and tell me that Mr. Hargitty is injured, and then you pull a gun on me.... Good Lord! You, Oscar? You're the one to blame for all the trouble these past weeks?"

"That's right. All that crazy reverend did was run off at the mouth. He never took no shot at you, or at that marshal fella."

"But why, Oscar? Why would you do such things? Haven't I been a decent employer?"

There was the sound of a blow, and Sir Alfred cried out sharply. "You tried to ruin the whole damned ranch!" Oscar said. "You came in here and threw away everything me and the boys worked for all those years! You had no right, no right at all! If this place belongs to anybody, it belongs to the fellas who poured their sweat and blood into it."

"You . . . you may be right," Sir Alfred said raggedly. "Perhaps I should have decided to continue the cattle operation after all. We . . . we could buy some beeves and rebuild the herd—"

"No need," Oscar cut in. "We've still got half the herd in a box canyon up in the hills. Not far from the place that rock slide almost caught you, in fact. You damned near stumbled right over it."

"You . . . you started the rock slide?"

"Couldn't have you ruinin' everything."

"And that's when you decided to kill me and take over the ranch." Sir Alfred spoke with certainty.

"I don't much like the idea," said Oscar, "but it seems like the only fair way to do things."

"Fair? You call murder fair?"

Oscar didn't answer that directly. He said, "Nobody'll know it was murder. You're goin' to slip and hit your head while you're climbin' into that pool. Then you'll drown in it. Nobody'll ever think it was anything but an accident, especially since Jones is in jail charged with tryin' to bushwhack you. Now, turn around and start takin' your clothes off."

"No one will ever believe this was an accident," Sir Alfred said desperately. "When Marshal Long hears that I'm dead, he'll be suspicious and return to get to the bottom of this—"

"That lawman's not gettin' to the bottom of anything except a shallow grave," said Oscar. "He's probably there already. I left him up in the canyon for Jed and the other boys to get rid of."

Emmaline had been standing as still as a statue as she listened to the two men talk, frozen in place by horror as she listened to Oscar explain his villainy. Now, however, as Oscar mentioned so casually that Custis was probably dead, murdered by his associates, the horror Emmaline felt was suddenly replaced by something else. Rage shot through her, and without thinking about what she was doing, she lunged around the hedge that screened her from Oscar and Sir Alfred. With a furious shout, she struck at Oscar's head with the only weapon she had handy.

The handbag that was always with her, the handbag that contained the Baumhofer Cranium.

Chapter 17

Longarm reined in as he reached the stable. There in the corral was a horse that looked freshly ridden. He swung down from the back of the chestnut and slipped between the bars of the pen, approaching the horse and laying a hand on its flank. Warm and still a little sweaty. Oscar hadn't even taken the time to rub down his mount when he returned to Briarcliff Manor. He'd had other, more urgent things to do.

Such as murdering Sir Alfred Brundage, thought Longarm.

Quickly, Longarm left the corral and started through the garden on foot. He didn't know how Oscar planned to go about killing Sir Alfred, but Longarm knew he had to get to the Englishman as quickly as possible. He just hoped he wasn't too late already.

He had gone only a few yards when the quiet of the night was suddenly shattered by a yell.

That sounded like a woman, Longarm thought as he broke into a run. Even worse, it had sounded like Emmaline, he realized.

He skidded around a corner in the mazelike hedges in time to see a knot of struggling figures on the flagstones next to one of the mineral baths. Longarm's keen eyes picked out three people in the moonlight: Oscar, Sir Alfred, and Emmaline. Emmaline was flailing at Oscar's head with something while Sir Alfred had latched onto his gun arm and was holding on to it like a bulldog. Oscar slammed a punch with his other hand into Sir Alfred's face and knocked him loose, then backhanded him with the six-shooter. Sir Alfred stumbled and fell.

Longarm palmed out his Colt and shouted, "Oscar! Drop it!"

Oscar reacted quickly, twisting toward Longarm at the same time as he lunged so that Emmaline was between him and the lawman. Oscar's left arm snaked around Emmaline's neck and jerked her back against him. Using her as a shield, he stuck his right arm under hers and thrust his revolver toward Longarm.

"Long!" Oscar exclaimed. "Damn it, you can't be here! You're—"

"Dead?" said Longarm. "Not hardly, but Jed and a couple more of your boys are. Drop your gun, Oscar. It's all over."

A wild laugh came from Oscar. "I don't reckon so. You drop your gun, or I'll kill Dr. Colton."

"You hurt her and you'll be shaking hands with the Devil about half a second later," Longarm warned him.

"Maybe, but she'll still be dead."

Longarm sighed, but the barrel of his gun remained rock-steady. "Looks like we got us a standoff, Oscar."

"Nope, because I got the lady here. Might as well fold while you still got the chance, Long."

Longarm hesitated, remembering how Oscar had come close to shooting him back in the cabin but had ultimately left the job to Jed. Unwisely, as it had turned out. He said, trying to sound confident, "You won't shoot Dr. Colton, Oscar. You're a lot of things, but you ain't cold-blooded enough to kill a woman like that."

Oscar's hat had come off during the struggle, and his gray hair was askew. He glared over Emmaline's shoulder at Longarm and said, "Maybe I'm learnin'. Maybe you never should've pushed me into a corner."

Coldness rippled through Longarm at the dead sound of Oscar's voice. He had heard that tone before, in men who had decided that there was no way out, so they were going to take as many of their enemies down with them as they could. Longarm knew that in the next instant, Oscar might kill Emmaline and then risk everything on a shootout with him.

Sir Alfred came up off the flagstones and lunged at Oscar from behind, reaching around to grab the man's gun hand. Oscar's gun went off, but the slug ricocheted harmlessly off the flagstones. Longarm couldn't risk a shot, so he lunged forward, bounding across the distance between himself and Oscar and leaving his feet in a dive.

He crashed into them, knocking Emmaline and Sir Alfred to the sides. Oscar went over backwards into the mineral bath and took Longarm with him. Water flew high in a huge splash as the two men sprawled into the pool. Longarm had lost his gun in the collision, but he managed to get his hands on Oscar's throat. They rolled over and over under the water, scraping themselves on the stone steps of the bath, but Longarm kept his fingers locked around Oscar's neck.

The water pressed against his ears. He hadn't been able to catch a deep breath before going under, and he was already feeling a tightening around his chest as his lungs cried out for air. Oscar struggled wildly, kicking and thrashing and punching at him, but Longarm hung on for dear life. He arched his back and thrust his head up, searching for air, and with another splash, his head broke the surface of the pool. He gulped down a breath as his hands tightened even more around Oscar's neck.

Oscar's hands came up out of the water, empty. He had dropped his gun too. His fingers clawed at Longarm's face, searching for the lawman's eyes, but Longarm held his head high and braced himself against the steps. He forced Oscar even deeper under the water.

Gradually, Oscar's struggles became weaker. His hands dropped away from Longarm's face and fell limply back into the pool. Thinking that Oscar might be shamming, Longarm held on to him for a couple of minutes longer, minutes that seemed more like hours. Finally, when Longarm let go of Oscar, the man's body drifted away loosely. Longarm pulled himself backwards up the stone steps, water streaming from his sodden clothing.

"Custis!" Emmaline cried as he sprawled out onto the flagstones. She knelt beside him and hugged him, heedless of the fact that she was getting soaked too. "Oh, my God, Custis, are you all right?"

"Marshal Long?" Sir Alfred said anxiously as he knelt on Longarm's other side.

"I . . . I'm all right," Longarm eventually managed to gasp out. "Watch out for . . . Oscar."

"I hardly think we need to worry about him any longer," said Sir Alfred. "No one can survive that long underwater. He's dead, Marshal."

Longarm slipped an arm around Emmaline's waist. Now that he was out of the water, the night air was pretty chilly on his soaked body. He huddled against her warmth.

"Oh!" The sudden cry came from Emmaline. She pulled away from Longarm, leaving him feeling somehow abandoned. "The skull!" she exclaimed anxiously as she scrambled across the flagstones toward the handbag she had dropped earlier. "I used it to hit Oscar!"

Longarm pushed his dripping hair back out of his eyes as he watched her frantically snatch up the bag and open it with fumbling hands. The cry of disappointment that came from her told him what she had found inside. She went to her knees and leaned forward, hovering over the bag as she began to weep.

"It's in fragments," she said between sobs. "Thousands

and thousands of fragments. I'll never be able to put it back together."

Sir Alfred knelt beside her and patted her back. "There, there, my dear. You sacrificed the Baumhofer Cranium to save my life."

"I . . . I know." Emmaline managed to smile faintly. "And I don't regret that. But still . . ."

Longarm stood up, went to her side, and put a hand on her shoulder, trying not to drip on her as he did so. "Sir Alfred's right," he said. "I reckon that skull got busted up for a good cause. Losing it is one more thing you can mark down against Oscar's name."

"Yes," said Emmaline, "and I suppose he paid a bigger price, didn't he?"

Longarm glanced at the pool, where the surface of the water was calm again. "The biggest one of all," he said.

Billy Vail looked across the desk at Longarm and said severely, "We generally frown on arresting folks and throwing 'em in jail when we know they're innocent."

Longarm puffed on the cheroot and blew out a cloud of smoke, then said, "I reckon you're talking about Reverend Jones."

"He claims you mistreated him something fierce, Custis."

Longarm shrugged. "I figured it was all for a good cause, Billy. I had to make Oscar and Jed think they were in the clear so that I could get the evidence I needed against 'em. Of course, not everything worked out exactly the way I hoped it would, but . . ."

"But Sir Alfred's safe again, and the fellas who were trying to kill him are dead, except for those other two cowboys who took off like you thought they might."

"The sheriff down there in Trinidad followed their trail for a while, but he said he figured they were still running. Sir Alfred won't have to worry about them none."

Vail made a face and picked up a pen to scribble something on a paper in front of him. "I suppose that's it, then.

181

Mark Hanley's gone back home, so we don't have to nurse-maid him anymore, and I'll smooth over whatever yelling that reverend does. Just try not to arrest innocent folks in the future, Custis."

Longarm uncrossed his legs and stood up. "For what it's worth, Billy," he said, "Jones *was* damned annoying."

Vail made a sound that might have been a grunt, or might have been a laugh that he bit back.

"Got anything else on your plate I need to sop up right now?" asked Longarm.

"No, go on and get the hell out of here."

Longarm nodded. "I always try to follow orders, Billy, you know that."

This time, the strangled noise Vail was making as Longarm hurriedly left the office definitely wasn't laughter.

Chewing on his cheroot, Longarm walked out of the Federal Building and strolled down Colfax Avenue toward the hotel where Emmaline was staying. A smile curved his lips as he thought about her. She had gotten over the loss of the Baumhofer Cranium, at least to a certain extent, and since she no longer had to attend that scientific symposium in San Francisco, she had returned to Denver with him. "The least you can do," she had told him while they were making love in her hotel room the night before, "is keep me satisfied for a few days."

"Yes'm," Longarm had said as he thrust into her. "Always try to . . . uh! . . . oblige a lady, that's my motto."

Afterward, while they were lying cuddled together in the darkness, she had said, "I'll just have to make an even better archaeological discovery. I've heard rumors that somewhere in the Middle East there's an ancient buried tomb where the Ark of the Covenant is located. If I could find that . . ." She lifted herself on an elbow. "Why don't you come with me, Custis? It would be a grand adventure!"

"I reckon it would be at that," Longarm had said, cupping her bare breast and nuzzling the erect nipple. "But my work's here."

"Oh, yes," she had breathed as he began to suck harder on the pebbled bud of flesh. . . .

Now, as he knocked softly on the door of her hotel room, he wondered what she had in store for him today.

"It's open," she called.

Longarm turned the knob and stepped into the room, and he stopped short at what he saw spread out before him. His mouth went dry, and it was a few seconds before he was able to say huskily, "Emmaline, I reckon you've gone and outdone yourself this time."

"Then you like it?" she asked from the bed.

"Like it?" echoed Longarm as he surveyed the trays arranged around her that had obviously been sent up from the hotel kitchen. His mouth began to water as he stared at the thick, pan-fried steaks and the mountains of German potatoes. Sir Alfred would have had a fit at the sight of all that unhealthful food.

But sometimes, Longarm thought as he closed the door behind him and started toward the bed, a man just had to live dangerously.

Watch for

LONGARM AND THE REDHEAD'S RANSOM

254th novel in the exciting LONGARM series
from Jove

Coming in January!

**Explore the exciting Old West with one
of the men who made it wild!**

JAKE LOGAN
TODAY'S HOTTEST ACTION WESTERN!

J. R. ROBERTS
THE GUNSMITH

From the creators of Longarm!

BUSHWHACKERS

They were the most brutal gang of cutthroats ever assembled. And during the Civil War, they sought justice outside of the law—paying back every Yankee raid with one of their own. They rode hard, shot straight, and had their way with every willin' woman west of the Mississippi. No man could stop them. No woman could resist them. And no Yankee stood a chance of living when Quantrill's Raiders rode into town...

Win and Joe Coulter became the two most wanted men in the West. And they learned just how sweet—and deadly—revenge could be...

BUSHWHACKERS by B. J. Lanagan
0-515-12102-9/$4.99
BUSHWHACKERS #2: REBEL COUNTY
0-515-12142-8/$4.99
BUSHWHACKERS#3:
THE KILLING EDGE 0-515-12177-0/$4.99
BUSHWHACKERS #4:
THE DYING TOWN 0-515-12232-7/$4.99
BUSHWHACKERS #5:
MEXICAN STANDOFF 0-515-12263-7/$4.99
BUSHWHACKERS #6:
EPITAPH 0-515-12290-4/$4.99
BUSHWHACKERS #7:
A TIME FOR KILLING 0-515-12574-1/$4.99
BUSHWHACKERS #8:
DEATH PASS 0-515-12658-6/$4.99
BUSHWHACKERS #9:
HANGMAN'S DROP (1/00) 0-515-12731-0/$4.99

Prices slightly higher in Canada

Payable in U.S. funds only. No cash/COD accepted. Postage & handling: U.S./CAN. $2.75 for one book, $1.00 for each additional, not to exceed $6.75; Int'l $5.00 for one book, $1.00 each additional. We accept Visa, Amex, MC ($10.00 min.), checks ($15.00 fee for returned checks) and money orders. Call 800-788-6262 or 201-933-9292, fax 201-896-8569; refer to ad # 705 (10/99)

| Penguin Putnam Inc.
P.O. Box 12289, Dept. B
Newark, NJ 07101-5289
Please allow 4-6 weeks for delivery.
Foreign and Canadian delivery 6-8 weeks. | Bill my: ☐ Visa ☐ MasterCard ☐ Amex _____(expires)

Card# _____

Signature _____ |

Bill to:

Name _____

Address _____ City _____

State/ZIP _____ Daytime Phone # _____

Ship to:

Name _____ Book Total $ _____

Address _____ Applicable Sales Tax $ _____

City _____ Postage & Handling $ _____

State/ZIP _____ Total Amount Due $ _____

This offer subject to change without notice.